Manhattan Death Ballad

Manhattan Death Ballad

Maxim Jakubowski

First published by Telos Publishing 2025
139 Whitstable Road, Canterbury, Kent CT2 8EQ,
United Kingdom.

www.telos.co.uk

ISBN: 978-1-84583-253-7

Telos Publishing Ltd values feedback. Please e-mail any
comments you might have about this book to:
feedback@telos.co.uk

British Library Cataloguing in Publication Data.
A catalogue record for this book is available from the British
Library.

For D, with shame and love…

1
Moonlight Over Sitges

Leonard was drifting.

Since the loss of his wife to a terrible illness, he had entered a twilight realm from which joy and any kind of motivation had faded away one small increment at a time. Days passed by in a blur, hours ticking over in utter silence only broken by annoying call centre or phishing interruptions, and the newly-acquired routine of reading a few hours in bed after waking, late breakfast around 11, browsing the newspapers, preparing a meal for one and then TV and again bed had set in. He had a few friends but no wish to see them or socialise and after a while most of them gave up on him. Apathy suited him. Loneliness was wrapped around his soul like a tourniquet.

He awoke one day in June and looked outside the window only to feel a cloak of sadness falling across his mind like a shroud at the sight of the grey skies outside again, the cars driving by on the main road and the unkempt state of his house's front lawn and sighed. Shed a discreet tear in the privacy of his despair and then rushed upstairs to pack a suitcase. Half clothes, half books to read.

A handful of hours later his plane landed at Barcelona's El Prat airport.

Collecting his luggage from the carousel, he made his way through the green channel and found himself on the building's sidewalk right by a taxi stand. It was hot and the sky was blissfully blue. He asked the driver to take the coastal highway heading south. He'd called ahead from London and made the open-ended hotel reservation. He'd been to Sitges before and the place held too many memories but then very few places in the world didn't; they'd travelled a lot, although they'd never made it to Japan or Africa.

He was blissfully stretched across a towel draped across the hot sand on the nude beach, indecently sweating and feeling the warmth of the day feed his muted senses.

He'd briefly dozed off, the paperback he had been leafing through lying face down by his thigh, spine broken, its pages already yellowing. The beach had been almost empty when he had climbed down the rocks early in the morning. He opened his eyes. There were now more people around: a family with a baby in diapers sitting like a tiny Buddha on the edge of the water, waving a plastic blue rake in the air while his middle-aged parents were sprawled nearby under a brightly-coloured parasol keeping an eye on it while sipping from their water bottles.

Just a bit beyond them, close to the rocks, was the young woman.

She was naked.

As everyone in the proximity was, but her nudity was so unlike theirs.

It was brazen, impudent, a thing of sensuous beauty.

She was stretched out, legs indecently open to an impossible angle that allowed him, from his vantage point, to have a panoramic view of her private parts.

She was shaven smooth and her outer labia were clearly visible, framing her slit, a darker shade of pink, fleshy, sculpted, outrageously displayed with a sort of provocative pride which mirrored the shape of her lips painted scarlet, shining like a light across her face in harmony with the perfect curve of her breasts as she sat there reading. As much as her sexual characteristics were impossible to ignore, old habits made it impossible for him not to squint and try and decipher the book's title. A flash of recognition. A novel he had indeed read and knew well. He smiled. Felt an insidious tremor travelling through his lower stomach to his cock, triggered by that fortuitous combination of cunt and book. All the signs of the beginning of an unwelcomed erection. He quickly turned onto his stomach to shield it from view, amazed by the occurrence, seeing as it had been ages since he had been able to achieve a proper hard-on. It had also been nearly six years since he had last made love to a woman. His appetite ground down by circumstance as well as lack of opportunity or desire.

She was wearing an outsized man's Panama hat and he was unable to catch the colour of her eyes, the brim of the hat obscuring her face above her nose and painted lips.

He held his breath. Wiped his brow.

He wanted to sit up, somehow pretend to be reading too, but he was afraid the unexpected swelling of his penis would betray his interest.

It was a nude beach, but also one frequented by families and not a pick-up spot by any means.

For years he had been an unapologetic slave to his cock; as much as he had loved his wife, he had also enjoyed many affairs, his resolve never strong enough to turn down opportunities or the clarion call of female beauty and attraction. That terrifying call of lust and the wild that had so many times almost collapsed his life and that he had found so impossible to resist.

Had he believed in superstition or whichever religion's lore and been offered the opportunity once he passed on living again as an animal or another person or object, he had once joked he would have liked to come back as the singer and writer Leonard Cohen's cock! Think about it: Janis Joplin, Joni Mitchell, Jennifer Warnes, Rebecca de Mornay, the mythical Suzanne, Dominique Issermann and so many others equally famous and unknown! At least they shared a name, if not an appendage.

He had always been a man who liked women too much, although it had now been ages since desire had paid a call on his senses.

Time crawled by as the young woman kept on reading, her wonderfully indecent stance unchanged, as if inviting voyeurs to forensically examine her intimacy to their heart's content as she kept on enjoying her book and, possibly, laughing inside in the knowledge of their uninvited attentions. He knew he was not the only man on the beach who had taken notice of her and couldn't avoid peering, staring, checking her out. She was gently tanned all over, no hint of paler skin, her small nipples a quiet shade of maroon, her waist minuscule, the luminous outline of her body strongly delineated against the pitted greyness of the cliff's rocks.

It felt as if he had been covertly staring at her for ages, fortunately from behind his sunglasses, when she finally rose, set her book aside and stood up. She was taller than he had initially thought, and as she shed her hat, he saw she was blonde. Straight hair, parted down the middle, falling down to her shoulders

His heart skipped a beat. As if she ticked too many numbers on his imaginary want list!

She moved towards the sea, her stance steady and sporty, too fast for him to see what colour her eyes were from where he sat.

She moved into the water, her sumptuous arse slim and heart-shaped, neither too small or too large, swaying gently above her hips with every forward step, as if she was profoundly aware that every set of male eyes in the proximity was following her progress and was smiling inside at the effect she was having. Quite possibly, he guessed, women were following her movements too, either envious or admiring. A small wave broke against her midriff as she dived in and began to swim, a powerful stroke rapidly taking her to the line of the rocks dividing the beach from the portal area.

He could see her head bobbing in the distance on the surface of the sea; she had swum quite a long way out, further than he had ever done.

He had been planning to leave the beach and return to his hotel and catch a bite at one of the restaurants on the port's promenade. Some tapas maybe; nothing heavy. But he was intrigued enough by the young woman and decided to stay put. See how things would go. How would she dress; as much the measure of a woman as nudity; where she would head off too. The town? The port? The hill and its warren of villas and apartments?

He sat in the midday sun waiting for her to return from the sea; many of the families from earlier had already packed up, protesting kids in their wake. Her beach towel in every shade of the rainbow lay tangled in the sand held in place by the book she was reading, the hat overturned next to a small tote bag advertising a brand or product unknown to him. Now, he could no longer concentrate on the pages of his own book, a myriad thoughts racing through his distracted mind.

The sun was rising ever high in the blue sky, any shard of cloud long banished and a gentle breeze swept wavelets of heat across his skin. He spread some more high protection suntan cream across his nose, cheeks, shoulders and cock head. The particular etiquette of nude beaches, he guessed, with a hint of a private smile.

Finally, she emerged from the sea, her golden body dripping rivulets of water down her curves, paused for a moment, her feet adjusting to the temperature of the sand, and then strode towards her towel and possessions. She slowed as she was about to overtake his position, then looked down at him. Their eyes met. He hoped he was feigning indifference, but she knew otherwise. She stood there for a moment as if daring him to keep on looking her in the eyes, rather than indulge in gaping at her nude body. He held her gaze.

Now he saw her eyes were green. Sharp, mischievous, provocative. A deep green the shade of a dark, muddy pond.

She stood silently, her body language asking him 'What are you looking at?' as if she didn't know already.

'Hello,' he said, desperately struggling for something, the

right thing to say in these curious circumstances.

The hint of a smile coursed through her full lips, as she fully acknowledged his presence.

'That's a good book,' she said, pointing at the paperback sitting in his lap, concealing his cock from view. 'Practical too,' she continued, 'as it leaves me at a disadvantage. You can see all of me, but it's not reciprocated ...' Her eyes literally sparkled as she said that.

She spoke English with an accent he couldn't quite place. Certainly not from Britain, but again not quite American. Canadian maybe? But then he was no expert in US regional variations. At any rate, they spoke the same language which came as something of a relief. In what felt like a charged situation, at least they could express themselves with no risk of confusion.

He was still trying to elucidate whether she actually meant he should move the paperback away from his crotch and reveal himself, but was struggling with words and indecision. She noted his discomfort.

'Us girls can be voyeurs too, you know ...'

'It's an equal opportunity world,' he remarked in response as he pushed the paperback away from his lap. She smiled, gave his cock a rapid glance and opined 'Decent but nothing special,' with a gentle peal of laughter.

'If you're after size or adornments, you should move further East down the beach to the gay section,' he remarked. 'Purely as an observer, I'd say the variations in size and girth there are sometimes eye-watering and you have piercings and rings galore on open display there to complete the full penile smorgarsbord.'

'True,' she said, 'but it's a waste, don't you think, such splendid physiques and attributes but no use to us poor heterosexuals?'

'Can I be excused from answering that question. Take the fifth, as I think you would put it?'

'You're excused. But gallivanting about on a nude beach is such a perilous affair, don't you think? There should be an etiquette book about all the perils to avoid …'

'Or those you wouldn't mind succumbing to?'

That affectionate but mischievous hint of a smile again.

'I like the book you're reading,' she said, changing the subject of the conversation to his blessed relief as he was unsure how long he could sustain the verbal jousting and stay within the bounds of propriety, let alone avoid an erection as her body towered above him, all in curves, glossy beauty and shaven mound like a constant provocation for his already aroused senses. 'I think I've read all her books,' she said, referring to the author.

'I've read yours too,' he turned his head towards her neighbouring beach towel on which the broken-spined paperback lay open.

'A reader too. Wonderful! But you must have good eyesight,' she remarked, indicating the distance between their patches of beach. 'Which means you had noticed me before …'

'How could one not?' he smiled, relieved that the cat and mouse game she had deliberately set in motion was leading into less ambiguous territory. 'You were certainly unavoidable.'

'I'll take that as a compliment,' she stated, swivelling on one foot and walking back to her beach towel.

She leaned over and picked up her tote bag, pulling out random items of clothing from it, bending forward indecently so that his view of her backside was unrestricted and positively obscene. He gulped but couldn't pull his eyes away. She straightened out and pulled a thin white cotton dress over her shoulders and his unrestricted view of her body came to a sudden halt. The dress reached down to mid-thigh, highlighting the feline gait of her legs. He didn't know whether he felt disappointed or relieved, all kinds of contradictory thoughts swirling through his mind. He couldn't help but noticing, though, that she had not slipped on a pair of panties; did noting that sort of detail mean he was turning into a dirty old man, a respectable pervert?

'Ciao,' she shouted out as she walked away towards the steps leading off the beach, rather than climbing up through the rocks, the fastest way to the promenade.

It was all a bit abrupt, he reckoned, struggling with indecision. Should he call out to her, stay put and hope she would be here same time tomorrow, follow her even?

She was already halfway up the steep steps that led to the promontory that wound its way above the cliff, her direction still unknown, town or port? He grabbed his shorts and crumpled shirt, hastily slipped them on and gathered his water bottle, book and belongings and rushed across the sand. Follow her he would. What's the worst that could happen? He looked back at the bed of sand where she had sat, now a mess of footsteps, hoping she might have forgotten something thus providing him with an excuse, a justification for tailing her, but there was nothing to retrieve.

Fifty yards or so ahead she took the cliff road overlooking the sea, the whitewashed walls of the local cemetery to her right, moving towards San Sebastian beach and the town. He tried to keep his distance as she strode ahead, hoping she wouldn't turn her head back and spot him following in her wake. If she did so, how would he react: sheepishly smile like a holy fool, pretend it was a coincidence, evoke the laws of fate?

She walked down the esplanade and continued along the parapet that overlooked the town's family beach, ignoring the multitude of restaurants on the other side of the road and the appealing smell of food drifting across the area and turned left at the end, then began climbing the narrow street squeezed between the church and the museum. He slowed his own pace, distractedly trying to remember all the tradecraft tricks he had read about in the spy thrillers that formed his guilty reading pleasure. But then neither did she look back or pause to feign tying a shoelace or look at a window to check she wasn't being followed. There was nothing melodramatic about the situation: just a woman wearing no underwear being stalked by a man who should know better! As she emerged onto the small plaza in front of the church doors, overlooking the ocean, an old rusty canon from a past colonial war on silent display, he felt a moment of hesitation, of doubt. Damn it, the only reason he had gone to the nude beach in the first place was because it was the nearest to the hotel he was staying in, and in no way in the hope of feasting his eyes on naked women, let alone men!

She ambled down the main promenade, moving unhurriedly, gently swinging her tote bag against her side as she moved. There was a brusqueness about the way she walked despite her leisurely pace; a catwalk model she certainly wasn't as she dodged families, dogs, and unpredictable small children precariously holding ice creams. Then, as if changing her mind, she abruptly moved right, crossed the central section, descended the steps, and entered La Santa Maria Hotel on La Ribera. He halted and watched her disappear inside. It was better known as a popular seafood restaurant and dozens of tables were spread out alongside the façade of the building, with busy waiters navigating between them serving the customers under a cloth awning; there were still a fair number of folk still busy eating even though it was almost past lunchtime.

He now faced a dilemma. How long would she remain in her room before exiting again? Quick shower or lengthy siesta? Then another thought struck him: maybe she wasn't alone and there was someone waiting for her already in the room, a partner, a lover? Could she even be making love right now to a hypothetical stranger, fine sand from the beach still lodged between her toes, the sweat of the day still illuminating her skin?

Standing across from the hotel's terrace, he caught the smell of food and took a snap decision. He walked across and sat himself down at an empty table and asked a waiter for the menu. He was actually hungry. And the table he had chosen had a clear view of the hotel's doors so he could keep an eye out for her.

The service was slow, with the staff between shifts, and he was only a handful of spoonful's into his fish soup when the young woman from the beach walked out of the hotel. Her hair was still wet from a shower and she had changed into a pair of skinny jeans and a white T-shirt.

She noticed him immediately.

'What a coincidence,' she said.

He mumbled something with his mouth full, taken by surprise at the speed of her reappearance.

'Hmm, hmm …'

Her eyes sparkled with mischief.

There was something oddly familiar about her, but he knew they had never seen each other before. She looked a bit like the Swedish actress Rebecca Ferguson and a slightly older version of Ellie Rowsell, the singer in Wolf Alice.

'In that case, can I join you?'

'Absolutely. You'd be most welcome.'

She sat down, facing him across the table, picking up a piece of bread from his basket and idly nibbling away at it.

'I'm Meg. You?'

'Leonard.' It occurred to him he could have given a false name, and he didn't know why he hadn't lied.

'Should I call you Len or Lennie?'

'Please don't …'

'Deal … and I'm not Margaret, Megan or Meghan with an H either …'

Gut feeling told him she wasn't lying either. The name certainly suited her. This didn't feel like ordinary circumstances. Which she reminded him of the next time she spoke, while lazily perusing the menu an elderly waiter had brought along.

'Awkward, isn't it, meeting with our clothes on?'

He held her gaze, struggling for the right response, and was saved by the return of the waiter requesting her order. She went for the seafood linguine and a glass of the house white.

As he had failed to respond to her question, if it was even a question, she returned to the verbal fray. 'So are you a regular on the Balmins beach?'

'The utter truth? It was my first time. I only came to Sitges a couple of days back. But I have attended nude resorts before though; in France, parts of the Caribbean. I find it oddly liberating. What about you?'

'Part and parcel of my job. I'm here looking for a man. I was informed he often frequents the nude beach further to the right, the gay area. But it would have felt wrong sitting myself in their midst, though. So, I was observing at a distance, blending in you could say. Just waiting for my man.'

Leonard was unsure if she was joking or not.

Their main courses arrived. He squeezed lemon juice and sprinkled pepper across his calamari rings and she dug into her own dish with gusto.

'And you?' she asked. 'Vacation or what?'

'I'm sort of travelling. Biding my time, I suppose you could put it. Went to an airport and came here; they had seats left on the plane. It was a spur of the moment thing. Not even sure how long I will stay. So, what sort of job are you here for? Why are you looking out for this particular guy?'

'I've been assigned to kill him.'

He looked up from his plate to check whether the look on her face was malicious, but she was quite deadpan.

'You enjoy teasing people, don't you?'

'I do have a warped sense of humour, it's true' she admitted, 'but I am dead serious. I just happen to kill people for a living.'

'No?'

'Yes. Well, someone has to do it, and it pays well.'

'And parading your lovely parts on a nude beach forms a part of the job?'

'You could say so. Helps me blend in.'

'From my vantage I must say you in no way blended in. Quite the opposite in fact: you stood out. I know flattery will get me nowhere but you were the most beautiful woman on that beach.'

'But, for my intended target, I was a naked woman surrounded by other nude female bodies; being into men and cock, he will in all likelihood not have made a particular note of me.'

Maybe he should play along with her fantasy or the joke. 'So how many people have you killed?'

'That's for me to know and you to remain in ignorance of, I fear. A girl doesn't put out to a stranger on their first date, does she?'

'How did you come to be in such an unusual profession?'

'It's a long, boring story ...'

'Meaning you won't tell me?'

'I won't.'

The conversation had reached an awkward point. Should he continue playing her game or just give up on finding any truth in her words? What did he want from her, after all, beyond the animal attraction she had surprisingly triggered in his lower stomach? Was he ready to play with fire, as he was slowly feeling he was inch by inch moving onto dangerous ground, new ground previously unknown to him?

Her unkempt hair had now fully dried and the hint of curls forming made her look wild and enticing.

Oh, to know someone like her, physically, sexually ... to connect with that sharp mind inside that killer body ... Leonard sighed. Wiped his lips clean with the cloth napkin. It had been too long indeed since he had last lusted for a woman, and he welcomed those sensations with a shimmering sense of expectation.

'I know you followed me from the beach.' Meg stated upfront.

'I did,' he confessed.

'I'm so glad you're not denying the fact. I don't like men who lie or wallow in shallow pretence.'

'How could I not follow you? I'm all too aware you know the power someone like you, your body can exert on old fools like me.'

'I do.'

A long, weighted moment of silence, empty dishes on the table between them, a gentle breeze swaying across the restaurant's terrace. He almost anticipated what she was about to say, however improbable it was.

'So, help me kill Bogdan and you can have me ...'

'Bogdan?'

'That's his name.'

'How?'

'You can be the bait. He likes men and however much I might flaunt myself, I wouldn't catch his attention in a month of Sundays to lure him or deceive him.'

'I'm not gay.'

'Surely you've had thoughts, curiosity? What it would feel like, inside your mouth, you in his mouth, being penetrated? Don't deny it, it's natural. I'm told all men have those occasional thoughts. But you wouldn't have to go through with all the messy stuff. Just bring him to me or a dark place of your choice and I will do the rest.'

'Jeez ...' But she was right, there had been moments when he had wondered what it would be like with a guy, but they had been fleeting. To feel what a woman felt. He had never been close to doing something about it, quickly storing the wild speculation away.

Meg kept on staring at him, testing his resolve. He realised it was no longer a game.

'Is he a bad man?' he asked her.

'I assume so, but then I don't ask questions; the less you know the better in this line of work.'

Sometimes the road you take presents you with choices about the onward journey. He wouldn't call it opportunities. He was drifting, he was without joy. Leonard said yes to Meg,

'I haven't a clue how I should go about flirting with a guy. Anyway, who would desire me? I'm middle-aged and, as you have no doubt noticed, can't even flaunt the ghost of a sixpack,' he pointed out.

'It's a dance,' she remarked. 'No different than if he were a woman. Play hard to get one moment, and evasive the next. Tease. Smile. Look studiously thoughtful ... Straight men are always attractive to them. A challenge, I reckon.'

'Easy for you to say. You're no doubt a prima ballerina amongst such dancers.'

'Play it by ear; no harm in trying is there?'

The following morning, he descended the steps to the Balmins beach, but instead of laying down his towel where he first encountered Meg the previous day, he made his way a hundred meters further East to the crowded area by the rocks where the crowds of gay men congregated. He stripped, self-conscious of the fact he was no athlete or ephebe. He could see Meg in the distance, observing his actions. As if directing him from afar, her naked puppet controlled through invisible strings.

He sat down, pulled his book out of the rucksack and began to read, or at any rate pretending to do so, all too aware of the throng of nude men surrounding him like the red Indian tribes hemming in General Custer's men at his last stand. A festival of genitalia clouding his new-found horizon. All sizes, girths, shades and angles. Suffocating him and making him all too aware of his own shortcomings. The majority of them were outrageously Perma tanned, defined abs delineating their posture like alien exo-skeletons. And then there were the piercings ... and the cock rings ... The heavy, musky smell of masculinity was overwhelming. The last thing he now wanted was to be outed as a voyeur. He flashed back to their puzzling conversation of the previous day.

'So, you want me to lure him to my room?'

'Of course not. Bodies are cumbersome. Unless you can think of a practical way to get rid of the body after the act is done ...'

'Of course; I wasn't thinking.'

'No, you weren't. It's not like the movies, you know.'

'So?'

'It'll have to take place outside. Somewhere remote, empty. By the ocean. We can drag him out to sea afterwards.'

He glanced around him. Small groups were forming, men who already knew each other, while some were dipping their toes in the sea just a stone's throw away. When one or the other negligently looked at him, he responded with a non-committal nod of acknowledgment.

Bogdan was a heavy-set fellow, with slicked-back hair, a swimmer's broad shoulders and barrel-chested, small dark eyes set deep, stubbled chin and lips curling with cruelty. Unavoidably, he checked out his crotch. He was unfeasibly thick, more a lethal weapon than straightforward genitalia emerging from a thicket of ebony curls. He gulped at the mere idea of closer contact.

It took two days. A clumsy hesitation waltz of small talk, unsubtle hints, feather-like touches of fingers on flesh that felt to him like low-key electric shocks every time Bogdan's fingers lingered across the skin of his arm and, as he offered no resistance, his buttocks.

He knew he was playing a part but notwithstanding couldn't help thinking feverishly of how it would feel if he allowed the seduction to run its full course, speculating wildly about the sensation of being impaled on the rough man's merciless cock, or having to taste it. He was surprised that part of him was not opposed to the prospect although the thought of kissing another man was still a bridge he knew he would be unable to cross.

They shared meaningless conversations, drinks, jokes, swam together. Bogdan was from Albania and made it clear from the onset that he was undoubtedly the alpha male in their tentative flirtation. All the while, further down the beach, Meg watched them, an enigmatic smile shaping her lips, waving away the countless single men who attempted to start a conversation with her.

'How will you do it?' he had asked her. 'Do you have a gun?'

'Too dangerous, loud and anyway not the sort of thing I could smuggle into the country.'

'A knife?' he shuddered, as the image of a blade piercing soft flesh came to life on the screen of his mind.

'Maybe … We'll just have to improvise.'

Bogdan wanted to go dancing, but he excused himself because of a genuine bad knee and it was agreed they would share a meal before spending the night together. Bogdan knew a small bodega close to the railway station, away from the tourist beat, where a permanent cloud layer of smoke floated between ceiling and tables.

'You haven't done it often, have you?'

It was obvious. 'No,' he admitted.

'I'll be gentle with you at first,' Bogdan said. 'But I do like it a little rough. Later. I want to hear you moan as I mount you like a bitch …' He continued enumerating an obscene catalogue of what he wanted to do with him.

'My hotel room has rather thin walls, I fear,' he said. 'Maybe not there …'

Bogdan was briefly taken aback. 'I'm sharing an Airbnb with others, so is not suitable either.'

'What about the beach? Where we met. At night, it's empty and pretty isolated. In the darkness no one can see much from the top of the cliff?'

'Hmm … I like that.' Bogdan remarked.

It was what Meg and Leonard had planned.

Wavelets broke over the shore with metronomic regularity, like a faint, tinkling musical accompaniment to the dark night. It was fortuitously almost moonless.

Bogdan was slightly drunk and his hands couldn't keep away from Leonard's arse, as if wanting an early taste of his prey. They carefully made their way across the line of rocks that separated the nude beach area from the small cove next to it which could only be reached that way, the cliff offering no path to or from the top.

There was barely a whisper of breeze. It felt as if the whole world was suspended. Darkness, his nerves on the very edge, the Albanian's rank breath still reeking of wine just inches away from his face.

He knew, hoped that Meg was nearby, lurking, waiting, ready.

Bogdan stripped. Indicated he should too. He did so slowly.

Leonard felt the other's man hand grip his cock and squeeze it. It hurt. He leaned over towards him like a looming predator and he experienced a sense of panic.

'I don't kiss,' he squealed.

The Albanian laughed out loud and took a grip of his hair and tried to force him down to his knees in the damp sand, so that his mouth could pay homage to him. He could smell the pungent smell of urine, or was it ammonia, drifting closer to his nose, rising from the rough man's penis. Closed his eyes, bowing to the inevitable.

The grip of Bogdan's fist tightened on his hair and began forcing his whole head into his direction.

His heart was beating the wild fantastic. A mixture of terrible fear but also guilt and curiosity; a canvas of sensations he had never experienced previously in such nervous harmony.

Just as he was about to bow to the inevitable, there was movement behind his aggressor, and he heard him grunt as Meg swiftly circled his throat with a thick length of rope. Bogdan stumbled back and his sheer weight pushed Meg back and she must have loosened her hold on the improvised garrotte. A clumsy dance unwrapped on the sand as both tried to find their footing in the soft sand of the cove.

This was not going as planned, he thought; she should have used a rock or something heavy to at least weaken the Albanian before providing the coup de grace. Bogdan's features were twisted with surprise and rising anger as he realised he had been attacked by a mere female of the species. Meg fell back and the brute now towered above her. She wore black cargo pants and a similarly dark T-shirt, her silhouette blending in with the surrounding darkness. Bogdan grunted and turned his attention to her, now oblivious to Leonard's presence. He cautiously moved towards her, his breath halting, his fury unleashed.

A distant cloud floated with agonising slowness across the sliver of moon visible in the night sky, cloaking the whole scene in an aura of unreality. Leonard noticed she now held a thin switchblade in her hand as the big man surged towards her. They made contact. Bogdan had kicked her in the midriff just as she stabbed him in the lower stomach. He howled but did not falter and stood his ground. The wound must only have been superficial. Meg was bent over, and he kicked her again, in the arm and the knife went flying. She was now unprotected.

It was all happening too fast, he thought, even though it felt unreal, unfolding in slow motion.

He could now see the fear in the young woman's eyes. Still on his knees, he crawled quickly towards the rocky cliff, his hands running across the sharp surface, hoping to find a rock, a stone that could be easily dislodged.

He heard Bogdan kicking her again and her shriek of pain.

A fist-sized rock came loose.

He straightened out and rushed back towards the struggling couple and with all the strength he could summon hit the back of Bogdan's skull with the rock. For an instant the man froze, then bent over in pain.

'Go for the knife,' Meg shouted out.

Leonard looked down at the ground, and there was the blade she had previously used, just a few inches away from his naked foot. He picked it up and rushed towards the kneeling Albanian who had his back to him.

'Do it. Just do it,' she screamed out.

And Leonard cut Bogdan's throat.

He had killed a man.

It wasn't supposed to have happened this way.

Meg should have done it.

She was the self-confessed hitwoman, wasn't she?

'Thank you,' she said.

'Did I have a choice?'

'No; he would have killed both of us. First me, then you once he came to realise you were my accomplice and had deliberately lured him into the ambush.'

She was still kneeling, visibly in pain.

'Are you OK?' he asked.

'Just a couple of broken ribs, I think. I'll live.'

'Jeezus,' he sighed. 'So what now?'

'We dispose of the body.'

They pulled the dead man by his feet towards the water. It took both of them to manage his weight. Once in the sea, they ventured out until the water lapped at their waists and Bogdan's body began to float and they gave him one last shove and watched in the penumbra as the body drifted out further to sea, before they wearily returned to the shore.

He dressed in haste.

Her clothing was now soaking wet from neck to toe.

The clouds shifted, moonlight now pinning them down, two isolated figures standing in isolation in the sand, like dancers on a stage.

Sitges night.

In the distance, a cruise ship moved along the sea, no doubt transporting thousands of elderly passengers towards the gems of the Mediterranean. Little could any of them know that he had just committed a bloody murder just as they wined and dined.

'Your hotel is too far. You'll have to come to mine; it's just a 10 minute walk to the end of the port area.'

She agreed it was the practical thing to do.

The rivers of adrenalin running through him were beginning to ebb. Maybe the realisation of what he had just done would hit him later but, right now, he was curious to see how what remained of the night developed. A mixture of apprehension and curiosity and, yes, lust. He had never thought that the shedding of blood would make him feel that way, the finality of what he had been forced into doing. Or was it the prospect of finding himself alone with Meg in a hotel room?

2
Port Authority Angels

It was like a microcosm of society, but ever so slightly out of joint. Leonard thought of himself as a visitor from another planet watching, judging, wondering at the spectacle unfolding in his presence, a canvas of men and women in all sizes, shapes and destinations. The crowds crisscrossed the area by the stairs where he stood, like the round metal spheres in a pinball machine, pinging left and right, intersecting, all adopting various speeds to avoid colliding with each other in their haste or slowness.

There were businessmen in sober three-piece suits and shoes polished to perfection, women in trainers and summer dresses, teenagers with different levels of sophistication denoting Manhattan kids and new, tentative arrivals to the big city, their choice of attire a reflection of their status. Passengers arriving and others departing, dragging heavy cases behind them as they headed for the right coach. It came to him that it felt like being on a film set before the director shouts out 'Action!' and the principal actors and heroes make their appearance to the sound of Gershwin's 'Rhapsody in Blue', a piece of music which had always for him embodied the very essence and rhythm of New York City.

He remembered countless movies and TV series set here or somewhere similar reconstructed in the image of the Port Authority Terminal. The only elements missing were black pimps in outrageous, colourful regalia hunting down naïve girls from the mid-West arriving in Manhattan with a head full of dreams, skin like porcelain and soft, untrained bodies ready to be shaped into the ways of the world.

He spotted a sign leading to the left luggage lockers on the next floor and set off, barely evading a collision with a mother manoeuvring a pushchair carrying a bawling infant while clutching several plastic shopping bags with her other arm.

He reached the locker area and sought out the right number.

It was at eye level in the second bank of metal lockers.

He sighed.

It was wide open, empty, unused.

A dead end.

'What the fuck do I do now?'

Was it the end of this short road; a crazy improvisation that had seen him travelling to New York in vain?

His mind went back in time to the night of the murder. Only three days ago.

They had dragged themselves back from the sea where they had disposed of Bogdan's corpse. He was still stark naked, hopeful any splashes of blood had been washed away from his body but Meg had walked in fully dressed into the water and her clothing was now drenched.

What a sight we must make, he'd reflected; had there been anyone at the window of one of the few villas looming over the top of the cliff that overlooked the cove: a pale, naked man and a thin blonde whose black attire now stuck to her rangy silhouette like a negative shroud. Both breathless and panting, a curious ballet of guilt. But it was still out of season and most of the hill was unoccupied, while the quarter moon darkness would have acted as a filter to their crime.

They had furtively taken the steps up the hill and then down again to the port area and his hotel. There had been no one in attendance in reception and they took the elevator to his second floor room overlooking the swimming pool.

'Do you have anything I can change into?' Meg had asked.

She moved to the bathroom and he heard her wash the sea away from her skin in the shower.

They were of similar height although she was naturally

much slimmer and the sweatshirt and jeans he loaned her hanged loose on her frame.

'That's better,' she said. 'I'm exhausted. Sorry it didn't go down as I'd hoped, but you did well, Leonard. I owe you ...'

'So, what do they pay you by kill?' he asked, out of morbid curiosity.

'Why? Do you feel you're entitled to half of the spoils?'

'Not at all,' he spat out, almost indignant. 'I was just curious.'

She mentioned a healthy sum. 'And travel expenses ...' she added.

He nodded.

It was as if a world he had read about only in books was now coming into mundane existence. She hadn't dried her hair from the shower and he could see a mass of curls taking shape, like a halo slowly birthing above her head. His heart faltered. Why did this woman have such a strong effect on him? How did the sense of danger she projected so effortlessly overcome his natural caution?

Meg sat on the edge of the bed. He kept on silently staring at her.

'Unsurprisingly, Leonard, I don't feel I'm in any shape, mentally or bodily, to get up to much tonight; I hope you understand?'

'I share the feeling,' he agreed.

'I just want to sleep.'

'Me too.'

They awkwardly lay on the bed next to each other, fully dressed, and within seconds Meg was sleeping.

It took him much longer, conscious as he was of her presence at his side, of the warmth radiating outwards from her close body, of the undercurrents of questions and feelings bothering him deeply.

He didn't find the relief of sleep until nearer the following morning.

It was a grey day outside when he woke up to the sounds of cars revving as they parked outside the hotel below his open window.

He turned on his side and found Meg was gone. He rushed to the bathroom and only to discover she wasn't there either. She had left at some stage in the night without a word of farewell after he had finally succumbed to sleep.

He knew instantly that he would not see her again.

Later, he checked out the Santamaria hotel on the town's main promenade, but they had no knowledge of her. Although he knew it would be in vain, in late morning he walked over to Balmins Beach to check out whether she might be there, tanning herself again in the splendid altogether. Of course not. A murderer never goes back to the scene of the crime, do they? Although he had, but then he just didn't think of himself as one.

But once that last thought occurred to him, he had a moment of panic. Surely soon the Albanian's body would wash up somewhere close or just casually return to its initial point of submersion and it would become apparent he hadn't drowned. Meg had pocketed the lethal switchblade after he had done the deed, but it probably carried his fingerprints in addition to hers, which left him at the mercy of the whims of fate or whatever happened to her. Yes, he decided, the time was right for him to leave Sitges; get out of Dodge City soonest.

He was packing his few belongings when he noticed Meg had abandoned her wet clothes from the previous day in the bathtub. The black T-shirt and the cargo pants. They were still sodden which possibly explained her decision to cast them aside. Would it be safer to dispose of them, he wondered?

Maybe not in his own hotel room. He was about to stuff them in his beach tote bag with the intention of jettisoning them in some outside rubbish bin on his way to the train station, when a sudden streak of curiosity compelled him to check the pockets of Meg's cargo pants before.

In the left-hand pocket, scrunched up, still wet and lodged in the corner of the material were what appeared to be several pieces of discarded paper, now almost reduced to pulp.

He instinctively grabbed them.

Later, when he had time, he would try and dry them out and

identify their nature.

At El Prat airport he looked up at the wealth of destinations available to him. But before reaching a decision, he went to one of the bars to take time off and consider his situation. It was as if he was back to square one when he had arrived in Spain, both fancy free and lacking motivation. And all too painfully aware that all he was doing was running away from reality. And was also now a murderer. Albeit an accidental one in his prejudiced opinion.

He ordered an espresso. Maybe it would help him clear his mind. He felt a sneeze building in his sinuses; no wonder, with the time he had spent naked on the beach with Bogdan and then Meg and that lengthy, painful trek through the night tide.

He searched his pocket for a tissue and his fingers made contact with all that he had left of Meg's.

He carefully pulled the mess of crumpled wet paper apart, taking extreme care not to tear them further. Then he ironed them flat with the bottom of his cup. Only two small rectangles, like business cards.

The ink had faded badly on both of them.

In a spidery handwriting, the words 'Port Authority, Box 1944'.

The other feebly displayed the shadow of print and the name of a ballroom he was vaguely familiar with, located in Manhattan.

Both the clues Meg had inadvertently left behind pointed to New York.

It was an easy decision to reach.

Leonard moved over to one of the international airlines counters and checked out the next flights departing to either JFK or Newark.

He'd found himself a hotel three blocks away from Times Square. The place had seen better days, a tired lobby all muted colours and hiccupping electric bulbs lodged inside a high ceiling with peeling patches and in dire need of upkeep and a fresh coat of paint.

His room was no better, with the odd cockroach darting across the ledge of the window in the bathroom, which looked down on a deep, dark well surrounded by squat buildings and a mosaic of grey-bricked facades with bricked-in windows. The Algonquin was over the road, and from his bedroom window he could gaze at its well-lit façade and the parade of taxis halting outside it, disgorging the wild and the beautiful crowds, but it was well outside his budget should he have to remain in Manhattan for a lengthy period. At least he wouldn't be lonely, he guessed, and would soon be on first name terms with the cockroaches even if they lacked the wit of Dorothy Parker.

He spent his first week there criss-crossing the Manhattan grid of streets, changing direction on the whim of a mental throw of the dice, absorbing the atmosphere, the smells and noises of the city.

On the several occasions when he had visited the Big Apple with his wife, they had grown into the habit of staying in a boutique hotel in Greenwich Village overlooking Washington Square Park, but he was reluctant to travel that far south, fearful of the painful memories it might dredge up of their happier times together.

He knew it would take a long time to heal those wounds, recover that sense of joy that had once been part and parcel of his life.

He'd checked out the ballroom near Gramercy Park whose wet, soggy card he had salvaged from the pocket of Meg's sodden cargo pants, but it appeared it had been closed for a couple of years now and was partly boarded-up. However, a poster outside advertised the fact that it was due to re-open imminently, promising a 'dazzling return to the Jazz Age' with extraordinary evenings full of glamour and old-fashioned special events. But no specific date. He would bide his time, he decided.

He thought a lot about Meg and what had happened and it now felt like a dream, or was it a nightmare? Somehow he had no regrets but nonetheless was amazed at how his instincts had so easily taken over and he had killed a man in cold blood at the instigation of a woman he barely knew. Prior to Sitges, he never had an inkling as to how easy it would be to cross the line. Become a murderer. The funny thing was that he still felt the same man, as if nothing about his basic nature had changed.

And now so many thoughts surfed across his brain.

Could he do it again?

How did Meg become a hit woman?

What had he really felt at that moment when he was on the brink of leaving his heterosexuality behind?

It was confusing. Damn so.

In the meantime, he cruised the New York streets. Neither a tourist nor a local, a man out of sorts, unremarkable in looks, maybe a little overweight and seldom smiling; if only they knew, he thought as he made his way through crowds of office workers and commuters oblivious to his darkest secrets. But what does a murderer look like?

He had read nothing in the daily newspapers he had picked up since about a body washing up on the Spanish seashore with its throat cleanly cut, but then it wasn't the sort of news to make the headlines, let alone as it had occurred a continent away and American media clearly had little interest in what happened beyond its borders. Was he maybe a suspect in a faraway investigation? Could it reach him here through Interpol or whatever channel? And what about Meg? Were they both the subject of investigation or was it just him who might be the object of some international pursuit?

Somehow he kept on returning to the Port Authority; something about the hustle and bustle, the diversity of folk making their way through its doors and the thousand and one stories he could imagine for each and every one. He liked watching people and conjuring reasons for their presence here;

what they might have been doing yesterday, what they were also running from; what their futures held. This, purely as an observer as he had no wish to be a puppet master, to have any effect on their fate. No doubt their stories were prosaic and lacking in distinction or drama, but for a moment they were the heroes of their own life, their own private movie.

Was that young girl in the calico dress almost on the verge of tears fleeing an abusive relationship or a mid-West religious sect? Was that skinny guy with long hair wearing skintight black leather trousers soon to attend an audition to be a drummer in a heavy metal band? So many possibilities. Each one a possible book or movie.

Tales of Manhattan.

Of course, he had stories of his own.

He had not always been a faithful husband, unable to resist temptation. Even more so in New York on the occasion of past trips here alone, or to compound his infamy when he had arranged to bring women here to illicitly meet up with him.

There was Pamela, the wife of an Eastern European free jazz saxophonist whose moment of fame had long passed. They had met at a book launch and were fucking in his hotel room barely two hours later. The fact that she was not a blonde and his preferred type mattered not. When lust is released, he had no shame succumbing to its temptations. He would keep on meeting her on successive business trips, as her marriage was on and off and her husband was often away on tour. Carved deep into his memories was the time they were making love on a sofa in the front room of the apartment she shared near Columbia with a book publicist friend and Bruce Springsteen's 'Candy's Room' played on repeat on the record player and they were interrupted in mid-fuck by her returning flatmate who had looked down at the two of them rutting and barely raised a smile.

To his great shame he could no longer remember the name of the Baltimore banking executive he had met at a conference in St Paul, Minnesota, and taken to his bed. She was impeccably dressed as befitted her situation but once he had undressed her, he couldn't help noting that her underpants were torn and grey. She joined him on the occasion of his next business trip to New York and they had rough anal sex in the Gershwin Hotel, after finding out they now had little of import to say to each other.

He'd also brought Aida, the ardent Lithuanian woman who lived in Holland with a garage owner and whom he'd met online, to America on two occasions. Once to New Orleans, where he suspected she'd cheated on him with another local online friend, while he was out working; and another time to New York and the Gershwin. They had spent many hours in his room as the weather outside was so bracingly cold. They quarrelled a lot and she had no interest in the city and baulked every time he took her out sightseeing in an attempt to get her to love this wonderful, bizarre, crazy place, from the lights and erstwhile fleshpots surrounding Times Square to the lackadaisical charm of the Village. He was uncertain whether that had been their last trip together. The highlight had been when she had spontaneously given him a blow-job in one of toilets at the Metropolitan. Aida died of cancer some years later, bitter and angry at him, vehemently rejecting his sympathy and full of desperate rage when he suggested they meet one last time so he at least could hold her hand and express the extent of his sadness. But she would have none of it.

And then there was Giulia.

Ah, Giulia!

The affair that almost broke his heart into a million pieces.

She was much too young for him.

Which made Leonard feel atrociously guilty but also saw him falling desperately in love with her.

Yes, you can love two women at the same time, in different ways. He never ceased to love his wife.

Giulia was Italian, hailed from Rome and a family of medics, and was studying on an exchange year in Barcelona. They had already been seeing each other for a whole passionate year, he flying to Rome on some pretext, she coming to London while his wife was herself overseas, or meeting at conferences or film festivals.

He was staying on Washington Square and she was to join him the day following his arrival in New York. He had all sorts of plans, none more important (aside from the wonderful sex, of course) than walking the city streets and seeing Manhattan through her eyes. It would be her first time here, and he was also in love with her enthusiasm, her lust for life, the energy she radiated put him to shame and made him feel so old, and inappropriate. Then she missed her flight from Barcelona and rang him in tears; she'd left her passport on a table at the bar where she been killing time awaiting her call and by the time she had returned for it, boarding had already taken place! She was so sorry they would have less time together than planned and would now be delayed by a day.

Eventually she arrived.

She had told her mother back in Rome that she was visiting a boyfriend in America and her mother had gifted her with a beautiful blue silk night dress so that she could look at her best. Little did her mother know she was meeting a married man more than twice her age!

Four days.

Divided between his bed and endless walks up and down the New York canyons, watching her eyes so wide open with wonder; Japanese and Italian food in small, cosy restaurants on Bleecker and Sullivan Street. A movie at the Angelika, on the corner of Mercer and Houston. Roaming second-hand bookstores in search of rare books for him or titles he felt she should read and wanted to gift her. Picking up snacks from the 24 hours bodegas which they would later feast on in bed as they caught their breath between orgasms and caresses. Her easy nudity as she moved from bedroom to bathroom, her mass of jet-black curls, the dark delta of her intimacy, the words she would mutter, in Italian or in English, while he was inside her, that faraway look in her eyes when she gazed at him, full of questions and doubts but also, he knew, adoration. They both knew all too well, of course that their affair could have no future, but they wanted this moment to endure, last as long as it could, hidden from reality, from their other lives.

'Whatever happens,' Giulia once said, 'I will always hold a piece of you in my heart.'

He could not recall if this was in Washington Square, the stone city to the north of Rome or in Barcelona.

She had, to his utter despair, decided to call the affair off before he had the opportunity to bring her to New Orlans, realising it was a dead-end road and the longer it lasted, the more grief they would attract.

Giulia, he remembered with a heavy heart, was also the only woman he had known who would sometimes cry, shed a gentle tear when she came, her eyes misting as he looked down at her, their bodies still so intimately connected, a thin sheen of sweat still glazing their skin as their limbs and parts remained intertwined and reality reluctantly dawned as the lust finally receded a little.

Bittersweet memories of her taking refuge in a corner of the hotel bar after he had needed a few minutes in private to phone his wife back in London, nursing her frustration at the fact he could not be hers 100% of the time; yet a further indication that they were rushing headlong down a one-way street.

Holding hands in public along La Guardia Place and buying luscious strawberries to bite on later as they sheltered naked between the sheets in their hotel room and its narrow bed overlooked by moody black and white framed photographs of Hollywood legends; catching a movie at the Landmark, hands and fingers indecently active in the darkness; the inevitable visit to Katz's Delicatessen on East Houston for mountainous salt beef sandwiches; an insight into his own culinary roots lunching at Veselka's Ukrainian restaurant on 2nd Avenue in the East Village to introduce her to pierogis, or as she opined just a Jewish version of raviolis; checking out the latest laptops in a computer store on West 23rd Street where you could pick Pepsi Cola bottles from dispensing machines while you browsed, this at a time when

US prices for hardware were so much cheaper than European ones thanks to a favourable exchange rate; rushing down Greenwich Avenue at midnight through the biting cold towards the harbour of their bed. Leonard remembered every street and avenue they had walked along with absolute clarity and a surfeit of regret. 'Four Days with Giulia': an impossible romance, illicit, improbable, poignant to be sure and memories that would have to last him forever. Images of her, words she had said, whispered in his ears, all that was now left to him. Was it already over 20 years ago? She was now married to an investigative journalist in Rome but was no longer visible on social media; maybe she now had children of her own, not that he truly wanted to know.

And he was now back in Manhattan, searching for ghosts past and present.

Giulia.

Meg.

His past and his present, like one map of New York superposed over another but reluctant to give up its dark secrets. A distorted hall of mirrors, a grid of his failures.

Like a clueless character in a Samuel Beckett play, he sat on a hard metal bench by the ramp in the Port Authority again, watching the people go by without quite knowing the purpose of his being here, waiting for angels to appear who could like a priest in a confessional box absolve him of his past sins. But, at the same time, part of him protested that they were not sinful, just unbound expressions of love, of lust, of longing, maybe also of desperation.

The strong smell of gasoline reached his nostrils as another arriving coach with a sputtering engine slotted into its designated parking spot. It was for a brief moment, so strong he felt like retching. He almost abandoned his seat, but the odour quickly faded and he continued watching the disembarking passengers as they found their bearings and moved on into the city, disgorged like cattle, their heads held high ready to conquer this new world.

His attention was drawn to a girl, whose backpack looked too heavy for her, casting around, hesitant, nervous, visibly in some state of discomfort as if the open maws of Manhattan were not as advertised, let alone to her taste. She wore a short brown leather skirt that skirted her knees, a red cotton shirt buttoned all the way up to her throat, and her auburn hair was braided as it fell to her shoulders. She looked like an exile from a 1940s movie, corn-fed, and provocatively innocent, tall and gawky She held a crumpled map of Manhattan in her right hand and consulted it feverishly, visibly unsettled by the teeming crowds rushing across from her, everyone with a destination in mind, hurrying, busy, while she was visibly glued to the spot. She looked up and noticed Leonard on his bench. Took a few steps towards him,

'Can you help me?' A strong mid-West accent.

'If I can ...'

The young woman appeared puzzled, not expecting his own un-American accent.

'You're not from New York either?'

'But I know the city well,' he said, almost apologetically.

'How far is Delancey Street from here,' she asked. 'I have a girlfriend who's putting me up on her couch there until I can find something of my own.'

'Quite a trek. You'd be advised to take the subway or a bus,' he suggested.

'I'm on a strict budget until I find work,' she remarked.

'Have you anything lined up?'

'I have a friend who told me the Continental Ballroom is reopening soon and have vacancies for taxi dancers ... I'm a good dancer. I thought I'd give it a try.'

The Continental Ballroom. The place he'd checked out. The card Meg had left behind.

'Taxi dancer? Is that like that film about the dance marathons, where you dance until you collapse and the winner takes all? Risky to put all your eggs in one basket, no?'

He recalled it was also a book he had read decades ago.

'I've seen the movie too,' she said. 'No. You sell tickets and men can dance with you. It's all very above board, I'm told,' she assured him.

'Oh, then …'

He was tempted to offer the young woman a lift in a cab, but demurred; it would have felt awkward sitting here in the Port Authority Terminal looking out for vulnerable arrivals like a pimp on the make from the glory days of Times Square at its licentious best. But he could spare a few bucks. He offered her a five-dollar bill, suggesting she take the subway. 'That should get you there. But you'll have to ask someone else what line to take …'

'That's so kind of you. Really.'

'Good luck.'

'Once I'm working at the Continental, I'll be happy to offer you a dance for free,' she added.

'I've never been much of a dancer. But I might well take you up on it.'

She straightened up, her back now supporting the whole weight of her rucksack again and stepped away towards the nearest exit onto 42nd Street.

He watched her disappear in the distance.

And sighed, realising he'd never even asked her for her name. Nor had she asked for his.

He was back at the cockroach hotel, nursing his feet in a bathtub full of lukewarm water. He had been walking all day. And the day before that, His left knee, which had been dodgy for some time since a stupid fall back home, was hurting every time he bent it or put pressure on it.

The phone in the adjoining bedroom rang. No one was aware he was staying here, let alone in the city, and he knew it must be ringing by mistake. Someone dialling a wrong number, no doubt. He didn't want to stop soaking his tired feet. Eventually, it stopped ringing and he returned to his idle thoughts.

An hour later, as he was munching on a chocolate bar and regretting the fact that American chocolate was so less tasty than English one, the telephone rang again.

This time, he bothered picking up.

It was reception. Someone had left an envelope for him. There was no one on duty right now to bring it up to his floor, but he was welcome to come down to the lobby and pick the letter up.

The receptionist, who had a Jamaican accent, promptly hung up on him before he could say anything. He had not advised anyone he knew that he was either in New York, nor staying here. Surely it must be some mistake?

Reception must be confusing him for someone else.

He hadn't planned to go out again today, and was mooching around in his undergarments but, after some amount of deliberation, finally slipped on a pair of trousers, pocketed his room key and made his way down the long corridor to the elevator.

The receptionist on night duty wore his hair rasta-style and a long, multi-coloured scarf was wrapped round his neck, even though the lobby area's heat was raised to tropical levels.

He was handed a white envelope.

It was definitely his name typed across it. In capital letters.

He asked the receptionist 'Do you know who delivered it?' but was informed he had only just come on to the night shift and it had arrived before, when one of the day staff had been on duty. Leonard guessed that explained the initial telephone call to his room.

Back upstairs a few minutes later, he carefully opened the envelope, cutting across the top with a pair of tweezers.

It contained a single sheet of paper.

Across which someone had typed, again capital letters:

'WE WERE MOST IMPRESSED BY THE WAY YOU REACTED IN SPAIN. SHOULD YOU WISH TO EXPLORE FURTHER WORK IN THIS PARTICULAR FIELD, WE WOULD BE GLAD TO ENTERTAIN THE PROSPECT OF EMPLOYING YOUR SERVICES'

A telephone number followed.

His first thought was that Meg had somehow located him and this was her sardonic way of making contact again.

But what about the 'we'?

Not that he had managed to get the opportunity to know her well enough, but it didn't sound like the sort of thing she would write or do to play a joke on him. But there was undeniably a connection to her. No one else could know what had occurred on Balmins beach.

He turned the sheet of paper over and over as well as the now empty envelope, in search of some clue, some further explanation for its existence.

Leonard was puzzled.

But didn't wish to act harshly or prematurely and decided he would take his time to respond before calling the number, or whether he would at all.

His swirling thoughts would have calmed down by the following morning, he reckoned.

An insidious voice, however, was playing cat and mouse with him, already suggesting he would prove incapable of not taking up the opportunity and calling the mysterious number eventually, however long he delayed the decision.

After all, tomorrow was another day.

3
The Taxi Dancers of Midtown

It's the loneliness that kills you.

The empty bed and empty room, the absence of a warm body by your side throughout the night. A human being with whom you discourse about nothing, share sights, thoughts, feelings.

He often displayed a façade of indifference, of disinterest which many people mistook for a lack of empathy, but he had long ago adopted the disguise as a way of establishing a frontier, a borderline separating the new him from his old self. When Meg had enquired about his name, he had briefly been tempted to lie, vaguely fearful she might have made a connection to the books he had written. Not that he had that many readers, to tell the truth ... But then how many things truly made sense in life?

He took to the streets mid-morning, first intent on visiting the bagel joint two blocks north for his lox and cream cheese breakfast. His mind was still debating whether to call the telephone number or not and if so, when? He didn't want to appear overly hasty. Later in the day his wanderings took him south of the Garment District and he found himself on the same pavement as the Continental Ballroom. The stone façade had now been cleaned of graffiti and the old posters had been stripped away, with the announcement of the imminent re-opening of the place plastered across the newly-varnished wooden doors of the emporium. The names of various bands and singers he had never heard of were listed, as was the 'long-awaited return of the taxi dancers to the big city' and later in the month the rebirth of the grand tradition of the dance marathon with mighty cash prizes promised for the hardy future winners, who were invited to put their names down as soon as possible before the complement was full.

Leonard smiled, his mind reflecting on how unglamorous his memories of the dance marathon in the movie were. But he was curious how it would unfold and resolved to visit when the time came.

He changed direction and was soon passing by Grand Central and was briefly tempted to visit the Oyster Bar, but realised he was still too full of the breakfast bagel he had eaten earlier. He descended the steps from 42nd Street and found himself on the Main Concourse, looking up at the splendour of the high ceiling and the way it reflected the outside light of the day.

There was a bank of public phones and he approached them, pulling the puzzling message with the telephone number from his trouser pocket and fumbled for a quarter. He dialled the number. It rang four times, and he was impatiently about to hang up when the ringtone broke off and a male voice said 'Yes?'. As if stung, Leonard set the receiver down. Had he somehow been expecting a female voice? Meg's?

He caught his breath, waves of anxiety coursing through him, his nerves on edge. He wasn't ready, he knew. He would try later, tomorrow or the day after. He couldn't, knowing his nature, not do so eventually. But he was aware he would have to be ready for the path it might launch him on, the consequences.

He exited Grand Central and lost himself in the teeming late-lunch hour maelstrom of commuters.

There were busy crowds milling about and heavy-set bouncers with mile-long stares guarding the Continental's front doors as he arrived. He hadn't given much thought as to what to wear but had instinctively gone for smart casual. A blue button-down Oxford shirt and pale beige pants with loafer shoes. He looked around and noted folk were showing off all sorts of vestimentary styles from boho to formal and all variations in between, and he at least didn't stand out too much. He'd never been a designer trainer sort of guy; thinking anyone over 30 or thereabouts looked a tad dubious in them! He waved his ticket and was ushered in.

The lobby was buzzing with excitement, voices loud and shrill, strands of music holding a steady rhythm, fading in and out, teasing their way out of the main auditorium that lay beyond the heavy dark red curtains separating the areas. He had thought it advisable not to visit on the previous day's opening night as it would have likely proven too busy as well as uncharacteristic, with, he guessed, hordes of B-list personalities, press, show-offs and the jetsam and flotsam of Manhattan society high and low. He had no wish to be photographed on the sly. Still thought himself as a fugitive from justice.

The actual ballroom was cavernous and high-ceilinged. Even though recently refurbished, the architect had decided to retain the exposed brickwork at the back at the hall and a balcony circled the room, held up by steel beams. It was both brutalist and art deco in appearance and it took Leonard a moment to find his bearings as he took on the view. Very few people were dancing yet as seemingly incongruous Motown tunes came roaring out of the banks of loudspeakers attached to the circular balcony that overlooked the proceedings. The Temptations, Marvin Gaye, The Four Tops.

He'd ascertained earlier than an actual live band would be playing, but the elevated stage to the right of the immense wooden dance floor was still empty, which could explain the lack of energy still permeating the room. Early days still before the devils of dance were unleashed.

He headed for the bar, a marble-topped dark wood counter that ran the length of the back wall. Behind it a trio of barmen, two men and one young woman, in identical livery of white shirt and red bowtie, officiated. He ordered a drink and found a free seat in a nearby alcove, nursing the glass for half an hour, one sip at a time while he grew used to the increasingly busy environment, savouring the beverage's sharp sweetness.

There was an announcement on the tannoy; it was so loud and distorted that he was unable to make head or tails of it, but it generated a sense of expectation, in particular among the hordes of single men loitering on the edge of the dance floor. Some brusquely adjusted the angle of their neck ties while others hoisted their trousers up and tightened their belts an extra notch.

A thin curtain of beads in a corner of the auditorium was pulled aside and the musicians made their way towards the raised stage. First the drummer, and then the piano player and finally the brass and string sections. They all wore white tuxedoes, with a thin black silk stripe running down the side of their trousers. Their black shoes were polished to perfection, catching the lights scattered across the overhead gantry.

Once every musician was in position, the band's leader made his grand appearance, tall, ramrod straight, in identical attire, his grey hair slicked back, a thin pencil moustache, and shoes polished to mirror shades standards.

The musicians began arranging their partitions on their matching stands, each of which carried the Continental logo when a loud collective sigh surged like lightning amongst the waiting punters. Leonard followed their gaze to the curtain from which the musicians in the band had previously emerged, and through which a parade of young women were now entering the ballroom.

The promised taxi dancers.

Unlike the band, they were not uniformly dressed in identical attire, trouping out onto the dance floor as if in formation, pretty maids all in a row. They ranged from tall to minuscule, with every hair shade known to womanhood on display, including many variations that had evidently come straight from a bottle. It was more difficult, at first sight, to determine their ages, but they too covered a wide spectrum from adolescence to maturity, characterised most often by the amount of make-up each girl had used to make herself stand out amongst the crowd.

Leonard had not expected their varied outfits to be so

demure and quiet. No doubt, orders from above from the Continental management who wished to reassure the local licensing authorities that their establishment was respectable and above ground, peddling enjoyment and not sex, he assumed.

Shyly, some men began to come forward selecting a potential dance partner and handing her a ticket, before they moved together onto the dance floor. He realised he had purchased no such vouchers and peered around to find out where they could be acquired and spotted an older woman in a three-piece suit and of masculine allure, puffing away at a cigarillo, sitting in one of the alcoves with a metal box in which she was depositing the money exchanged for the vouchers she tore off a thick pad. Once upon a time in more seedy times, the dance tickets had been cheaper and the girls were known at the 10-cents-a-dance-gals. Now inflation had taken its toll and it cost five dollars.

His eyes were darting from one dancer to another. Had she found employment here?

Yes!

There she was, treading slowly, almost reluctant to look at some of the men seeking dance partners squarely in the eye. The young girl from the Port Authority.

She wore a red corsage, buttoned all the way up to her throat and cinched at the waist, along a beige, loose skirt held up by a thick black belt. The skirt ended just above her knee, showing off the contours of her legs. Sensible brown shoes completed the ensemble. None of the taxi dancers wore high heels, which he realised made sense. For each of them, it was going to be a long evening, hard on feet and legs.

Above her right ear, partially tucked away into her auburn curls was a white flower he couldn't name. Was it real or plastic, he wondered? At any rate, it suited her, projecting an image of innocence tinged with wholesomeness but tempered with a note of seductive vibrations.

A man approached her. He was at least three times her age, running to fat inside his old-fashioned tuxedo and was bald.

She smiled demurely at him and accepted his ticket and led him to the dance floor. The band were playing a Bryan Ferry song, which echoed Berlin in the 1930s but without its insidious sense of decadence.

Leonard watched them spin around. The older guy was a decent dancer, moving easily to the beat while the Port Authority girl was hesitant and unsure how to respond to his lead, in all likelihood more accustomed to modern dances and not the formality and desired elegance of ballroom patterns.

He turned round and walked over to the alcove where the bored-looking cashier was selling dance tickets and acquired half a dozen. They were not cheap.

And then waited for her to become free. Finally, three dances later, the older man in the tuxedo decided he was ready for another partner, bowed politely at her and moved away. He might have been much too old for her, but he had behaved impeccably; not once during their dance had his hands strayed from her waist or her shoulders and he had always allowed her space, not forcing his corpulent body too close for comfort.

'May I?'

She distractedly pocketed the ticket he was proffering, then looked up at him. At first there was no recognition, but then she realised he looked familiar, but couldn't place him with any form of certainty.

'Have we met before?'

'Yes.'

'Where?'

And before he could say more, a gentle smile crossed her lips.

'You're the man from the bus station! You were kind to me.'

He smiled back at her.

'I'm Leonard. I forgot to ask you for your name last week …'

'It's Helen,' she said. 'Helen Georgeson.'

'I remembered you mentioning you were hoping to find a

job here. I was curious, thought I'd come and check it out. I'm pleased you did find employment ...'

The band launched into their next song.

She took him by the hand and led him to the dance floor where couples were forming.

He knew already that she was not the most accomplished of dancers, but then neither was he, so there was no need to feel embarrassed by his halting performance and relative lack of coordination.

'It's an American Smooth,' she pointed out.

'Is it?' He tried to follow her moves, in no way ready to lead.

They tip-toed around. He could feel the mint on her breath and a gentle wave of heat radiating from her body. He was self-conscious, aware of his nervousness, fearful his hands would become all sweaty.

'You're English, aren't you?'

'Guilty. There's no way I can deny it, can I, every time I open my mouth?'

She laughed gently. 'Is that what they call the British sense of humour?'

'Absolutely. We have an obligation to crack at least one self-deprecating joke a day and, preferably, in the presence of American mid-West beauties.'

Following the music as best they could, they turned and turned in unison, and he felt a sense of giddiness. He hoped the next song wouldn't be an American Smooth.

With some unnecessary flourishes and a brief, strident trumpet solo the band reached the end of the song.

'I hope the next one is a waltz or something less fast,' he said, trying to hand her over another dance ticket. She brushed his hand away.

'I owe you a few,' Helen pointed out. 'The next few dances are on me.'

'But don't you get paid per dance? I wouldn't want to ...'

'I insist. You were the first person to show me some generosity when I reached New York. Anyway, I only get to keep a third or so of what the punters pay by ticket. The rest goes to the house.'

It turned out to be a waltz.

By the time it ended, Leonard was too tired to continue but suggested to Helen they possibly meet up when her evening ended. She readily agreed.

After a four and a half hours shift dancing, and a mass of tickets stuffed under her skirt's belt, Helen said she was famished and he suggested they go eat something at Veselka, which stayed open all hours of day and night and was a pleasant short walk away on this cool night. The restaurant was surprisingly busy and buzzing at one in the morning. He recommended the pierogi platter, which she agreed to sample. He chose likewise, settling for the meat and potato stuffing.

'So what made you want to leave Virginia?' he asked.

'You know; all sorts of things really. A cheating boyfriend, the tedium, the lack of opportunities, fancy dreams and all that.'

'And dancing?'

'I suppose it was either that or waitressing, and it felt like a cleaner choice. I've had it up to here working as a secretary or clerking at the town hall and I do find offices stifling, so that was right away a no-no.'

He nodded.

'What about you? What brings an Englishman to New York? I get the feeling you're not here on a vacation. Are you?'

'I'm not. I've done vacations and business trips; this time it's something different. I reckon you could say I'm on the run ...'

'From justice?' she raised an eyebrow. 'That's very romantic ...'

'No, not from justice,' he technically lied. 'From life, the past. It's complicated.'

'I like it,' she smiled. 'A man of secrets, then ...'

'I couldn't possibly comment. I just happen to be here in Manhattan, with no plans, wasting time or biding my time, depending on your point of view.'

'Don't you have a job or someone to go back to in England?'

'No.'

She took her first bite. 'This is damn delicious,' she said, her tongue wiping her lip clean from the sauce. 'I'd heard of the dish, but somehow knowing it was sort of Russian, was never overly curious about it.'

'I have Russian blood,' he pointed out, 'but it goes back three generations.'

'I thought there was something foreign about the way you looked.'

'Guilty as charged.'

The conversation paused as they ate.

'I didn't realise how hungry I was,' Helen remarked 'Dancing sure gives you an appetite.'

'I'm told the desserts are wonderful here, although I never partake. Not a cake or pudding sort of man. You're welcome to order some. It's on me.'

'Thanks, I might well do, but right now I'm enjoying these pierogi. So, what do you do all day long?'

He paused momentarily.

'I walk the New York streets. I watch people. Window shop. Breathe in the atmosphere. Spend time exploring the shelves of used bookstores. Sometimes catch a movie at the first afternoon performance when the theatres are almost empty and the smell of popcorn is not as overwhelming. I think a lot.'

What he didn't tell Helen is that every time he walked by a telephone along the street he had a moment of anguished hesitancy, torn between ignoring it and calling that number again in the realisation it might prove a point of no return.

'That's a lot of time doing nothing,' she remarked.

'It is indeed.'

He was attracted to Helen, although she was not the sort of woman he had ever fallen for in the past. It wasn't that she projected innocence, but he intuited that she was holy in her simplicity, that what one could see from the outside aligned with what lay hidden on the inside. She was bright but no intellectual, pretty but not aggressively so. Guileless. Almost the opposite of Meg and the many women who had preceded her, who projected a delicious, intoxicating sense of danger, temptation, complications. She was a woman with no secrets.

He walked her back to her Delancey Street apartment share from the restaurant, taking 2nd Avenue past St Mark's Place and then the Bowery. The streets were now almost empty and it felt as if they owned the city, or at any rate the East Village as they shuffled along, in no hurry, equally at ease chatting or enduring long silences.

He had briefly entertained the possibility of inviting her back to his hotel but had ruled against it. Although part of him screamed out silently for the sensation of a woman's body against his skin, on the other he was fearful of a possible new relationship. The thought alone could have been presumptuous anyway as he had no idea what she had in mind or sought out.

He left her at her door. She kissed him amicably on the cheek and walked in.

'You know where to find me,' Helen said.

He reckoned it was an invitation of sorts to see her again, although next time around he would feel better buying the dance and using up the tickets he had acquired this past evening the way they were intended.

There was another white envelope awaiting him at reception at his cockroach hotel. The desk was not even attended at this late hour of the night and anyone could have walked in off the streets. The missive was lodged in the thin, wooden compartment where his key was stored.

He took the rickety elevator up to his floor, entered his

room, slipped off his loafers, sat down on the corner of the bed and tore it open.

Again, a single sheet of A4 paper.

'SO?' and the telephone number was repeated.

The temptation to call the number was constantly at the back of his mind as he toyed with the two options on offer. To call or not to call.

But he was also a great procrastinator and now sought ways to avoid taking a decision.

Could he, instead, track down Meg?

She was like a phantom lady, albeit one whose nudity he had vicariously feasted on, but how could he even know if she was in America, let alone New York? After all, had it not sounded her accent was Canadian? Or was it? Maybe she had affected the accent only to deceive him in her not-so-subtle game of entrapment, a game he had willingly entered, thinking he was the one in control of the situation.

Which had left him holding the bloody switchblade in his hands and the body of the Albanian laying at his feet in the sand, in the shadow of a quarter moon.

He tried to recall their few conversations, seeking a clue to her background, any information she might have unwittingly provided and which he could act on.

Had the subject of New York even attracted a perfunctory mention? Was Meg even her real name?

There must be a connection, though: only she had witnessed what had happened and therefore must have some form of link to this telephone number now being repeatedly dangled in front of him.

He had no clue where to begin and it felt as if an offscreen clock was ticking away in the background and there was a deep, existential mystery he had to solve before the clock reached midnight and his time in this version of Death Row came up, with no magical reprieve in sight.

Like being the prisoner in a noir movie unfolding in front

of his eyes, with his hands tied behind his back. *Cherchez la femme fatale!*

It took him a long time to find sleep that night, even though all the dancing with Helen had sapped his energy and when that sweet relief came, it was tinged with strange dreams, many of which saw him running around in a circular motion, ever trying to break out of the demonic loop, but unable to do so with an increasing sense of panic taking hold of his bruised senses. He tossed and turned between the sheets. Oblivious to the sirens of passing police cars, so often the soundtrack of Manhattan nights. Both in life and in the movies.

Peace washed over him eventually and he slept until mid-morning of the following day.

His energy had returned and he was determined that the next 24 hours would not follow the perambulating path of the previous week and he would do, try something different, break his aimless routine in the hope of accomplishing something, even if it turned out to be meaningless.

He passed on breakfast, deliberately walked different streets, avoiding the wider expanses of Manhattan's avenues where the wind rushed through the artificial canyons created by the looming masses of tall skyscrapers hemming the traffic in.

He bypassed the Times Square area and eventually, heading south, found his way into the Meatpacking District, an area he had seldom explored previously. He was intending to continue to Tribeca, but it began to rain and he hastily took refuge in a small café close to the corner of a narrow street off the main beat, squeezed between a florist and a Goodwill store. The moment he passed the door, the comforting smell of coffee and fresh pastries swept over him with a sense of pleasant familiarity. He wasn't even much of a coffee drinker, but it felt reassuring to the senses. There was only a half dozen tables scattered across the narrow room, a counter behind which a couple of coffee machines stood and a thin sliver of natural light peered through a rectangular skylight while exposed beams gave the locale a rustic feel. The few customers all looked like regulars, sipping in silence, some reading newspapers or magazines. A young woman wearing headphones sat in a corner, a pram by her table, listening to her music and chilling out. The place felt out of time, like a shard of the 1950s inserted into the modern world, deliberately unfashionable and proud to be so.

He found a seat.

A middle-aged waitress, her hair in a tight bun and wearing a colourful apron came over to take his order.

'Welcome to Wanda's Café ...'

She leaned forward to fill his cup with coffee, but he shook his head and ordered a soda instead, making it clear he didn't want any ice with it. An ingrained old habit of his.

'Will that be all?'

'Yes. For now. Nice place,' he remarked. 'Are you Wanda?' He couldn't see any other staff mulling around and she didn't have a name badge.

'Oh no,' she smiled, as if she had never been asked the question a thousand times before. 'That was a previous owner. A long time ago. Before my time. I heard she moved to Seattle. I bought the place from a relative of hers.'

The child in the pram began softly crying and the woman slipped off her headphones, picked the baby out of the pram and, in a familiar bid to appease it, held it tight against her chest, its swaddled body rocked by her own slight back and forth movement. It quickly went quiet, and with the utmost delicacy she replaced the child between the thin blanket bleached of colour it slept under. The young woman left the headphones on the table, next to her cup of coffee, as if uncertain as to what to do next, lost in thought and when Leonard glanced at her, he saw that she too was now crying, her blue eyes misting up. It occurred to him she was not a nanny but must be the baby's actual mother. And looked so young and unready to shoulder such a burden.

He was uncertain how to react, but before he could say or do anything, the waitress had walked over to the adjoining table and handed the woman a napkin.

'It will be okay, Georgia,' she said. 'You'll see, it'll all turn out alright. I'll keep an eye on her if you want to leave her for a few minutes and use the bathroom.'

The young mother wiped her tears away, stood up slowly as if unsure of her equilibrium and made her way to the back, while the waitress stood protectively over the now silent pram.

'Poor thing,' she muttered.

There was a story there, but if felt rude to Leonard to intrude and ask questions. It was safer to steer clear of other people's problems right now.

But as he emptied his glass and made to leave, noting the rain outside had stopped, he knew he would return to Wanda's Café again.

Once on the street, he shivered. The sudden downpour had considerably lowered the outside temperature and the thin short sleeve shirt he was wearing was far from adequate, as were his deck shoes. He turned on his heels and made his way back uptown.

Like a magnet, The Continental Ballroom beckoned.

The taxi dancers had already been busy collecting tickets for a couple of hours and Helen visibly looked tired. Tonight, she was wearing a white silk blouse and a black pencil skirt, and what looked to Leonard like an amaryllis in her hair. 'The blouse and skirt are not mine,' she said. 'I borrowed them from my friend's wardrobe while she is away visiting relatives in Cedar Rapids.'

'It suits you.'

'Do you think so?'

'Very classy, elegant. Look, tonight I insist that you take my vouchers.'

'I was planning to. But I can only have you as dancing partner for two dances at a time; those are the new rules. I haven't had the problem but some men have been a tad too possessive of their dancing partners and the management have insisted we follow the rules to the letter.'

'I'm fine with it. I don't know how you do it; after a few circuits of the dance floor, I'm wiped out. So, the occasional rest will be more than welcome.'

He handed the first voucher over. She had a small black leather pouch at waist level in which she stuffed it.

It was midweek and a relatively quiet night. He paid for her services on a half dozen occasions, usually waiting for the band to start a slow number, unless she was already taken. She was wearing a perfume that delighted him, with notes of green and every time he took her hand and one or the other led, he took a deep breath and inhaled her scent anew with relish.

'Imagine'

'Begin the Beguine'

'Wicked Games'

'I am Sailing'

'Me and Bobby McGee'

'Gypsy Wife'

Their dance songs; their moments together.

As they came together and apart, he could feel her becoming closer, acclimating to him, the movements of her body finding a natural rhythm that stemmed from the mere contact of their fingertips and the increasing warmth coursing through their bodies.

The band left the stage.

She'd picked up her coat from the dancers' dressing-room and met him on the outside steps.

'It was a lovely evening,' she said.

'Truly enoyable.'

'You're a gentleman …'

'Flattery will get you everywhere.'

He was going to suggest a last coffee somewhere before they parted, but she spoke first, looking him straight in the eyes.

'Coffee at my place?'

'Won't your flatmate be asleep? Don't want to disturb her.'

'She's still away for a few more days,' she reminded him. He had forgotten.

He hadn't expected the invitation. Although he had toyed with the idea, but the prospect of her being introduced to the gentle squalor of his cockroach hotel had held him back.

'I'd love to.'

Their lonelinesses met. The first kiss was tender and lingering. His hand went down to her waist and gripped her. She offered no resistance.

'I'm not very experienced,' Helen whispered.

'I am, but it means nothing, you know. Every time should feel like the first time.'

He undid the side button of her pencil skirt and helped it to the floor. She wore white cotton underwear. Her hold-up flesh-coloured stockings reached to mid-thigh. His heart missed a beat.

'Must we keep the light on?' she asked.

'I would rather,' he responded. 'All the better to see you, as the big bad wolf said.'

'You're funny.'

'I have my moments. It comes with age, so it's a double-edged sword, so to speak.'

They kissed again, her tongue fluttering against his, tentative, exploring, wriggling itself through the barrier of his teeth, tasting him.

'I like it you're not a smoker,' she remarked as she pulled her white silk blouse over her head. Her white brassiere matched her underpants.

He loosened their embrace and got down on one knee and began unfurling the stockings down her leg and then delicately pulling the material across her feet. It felt like a ritual; one he had not performed in ages.

'The bedroom is over there,' Helen said, pointing to a door to their right.

Late the next morning, he woke up with the young woman next to him between the crumpled sheets, cradling herself like a child, her nudity now one of innocence regained, the faint trace of a smile on her pale pink lips, her skin shining white and immaculate. It had been ages since he had made love to a woman, and it felt like being born again. Leonard experienced a surge of hope against hope as he watched her chest rise and fall and rise again with every successive breath. He sighed. Laid his hand on her shoulders. Helen stirred.

'Do you want to get up and go have breakfast somewhere?' he suggested.

She half-opened her eyes. Recognised him, then closed them again.

'No,' she growled. 'I just want to keep on sleeping. Do you mind awfully?'

'Of course not.'

'Thank you,' he said.

'Likewise; thank you Lennie. It was lovely.' He didn't correct her.

It had been lovely indeed. As if years had been erased from his life, and some of the more painful memories obscured.

'Do you want me to come join you at the ballroom tonight?'

'It's my day off.'

'That's great. Lunch or dinner or both; spend some time together, walk in a park; just relax? I'll go change first though; back to pick you up by midday?'

'Sure.'

She closed her eyes and was lost to deep sleep again in an instant. He dressed in silence, fearful of waking her. Saw himself out. The streets were busy with commuters moving like automatons up and down the Avenues. He carved a way through the crowds and took the direction of West 44th St., treading the pavements with a newfound determination.

Yet again the lobby was deserted and there was no one in reception. He picked up his key.

As he opened the door to his room, an unfamiliar smell assaulted his nostrils, acrid, metallic, reminiscent of ammonia.

He pushed the door open and switched the light on.

There was someone on his bed.

Naked. Arms and legs akimbo. An obscene composition.

It was a woman, blonde, her hair pulled back and splayed across his pillow.

It was Meg.

A line of bright metal and blood red circled her throat.

Leonard held his breath, his heart beating wildly, waves of anxiety running through his bloodstream and reaching all the way to his nerve ends.

She was dead.

Her open eyes peered at him blindly, erased of personality, misted over, emotionless.

He hesitantly approached the bed and saw that she had been garrotted, the piano wire still embedded deep into her bruised flesh, a thin streak of blood below it now caking and turning brown. Her lips were open, her tongue peered out, bloated as if the hopeless vehicle of a final, desperate scream.

The sinister portrait macabre that slasher killers compose like works of art in bad books or movies.

He felt bile rise in the back of his throat and rushed to the toilet bowl and was violently sick.

His thoughts rushed in every conceivable direction as he tried to control his panic. He caught a reflection of his face in the bathroom mirror. He was whiter than snow, more a ghost than a living being.

But he was the one who was alive and it was Meg out there on the bed who was dead. Paused like a pornographic marionette, all her dignity stolen from her forever. Whoever had killed her and placed her this way was sending him a message, one he would never be able to forget.

Eventually, dabbing cold water all over his face and not even drying himself with a towel, he returned to the bedroom.

The sheet below her was wet, the damp patch radiating from her midriff. She must have urinated, lost her bowel control while she was being strangled with the wire, her legs then forced wide open at an impossible angle by the killer in his attempt at presenting Leonard with an indelible nature morte.

He felt sick again, but there was nothing left to throw up.

He pulled both sides of the bedsheet which was tucked into the mattress and draped it around her body. A small mercy. For him. For her.

Tried to collect his thoughts.

What could he do now?

Flee?

But there was nothing he could do with Meg's body. It wasn't Sitges; there was no sea at hand to dispose of her body. Room service would inevitably visit and discover her remains as he couldn't keep a non-disturb sign hanging outside the door forever.

In his sense of panic, all he could think of was to flee the hotel, Manhattan, America. He was paying his room upfront in cash, not by credit card, and had not registered as Leonard, but under another name which no one at reception had questioned.

He knew he couldn't go to the authorities and inform them outright that he had found the body in his room and had nothing to do with its demise. In the long run they would surely identify her, then establish the fact she had been in Spain at the same time and place he had been. Add the probable discovery of Bogdan's body and the coincidences would pile up.

Could he get away with it? Were there any genuine clues the police could follow once on the case?

He was finding it increasingly difficult to think straight.

The only thing he knew was he shouldn't delay any further was leaving the hotel.

He packed quickly and carefully, avoiding any stray glance at the shrouded shape on the bed and checking every drawer, cupboard, bathroom cabinet and wastepaper basket for anything that he might have discarded.

He hung the 'do not disturb' sign on the outside doorknob, uncertain how long it would deter whoever cleaned the rooms from entering it.

Once again, the reception desk was unmanned. He

dropped his key on the counter and noticed that since he had arrived only 30 mns before, someone had placed a white envelope in his compartment. He snatched it, and pulling his suitcase along rushed out of the hotel onto the street. There was a yellow cab outside the Algonquin on the other side of West 44th

He asked the driver to be taken to Central Park. Somewhere he could sit down and steal some thinking time, reconsider his options.

Caught in a traffic jam on 6th Avenue, he nervously tore the envelope open.

As usual, there was just a single sheet of A4 paper.

'NEED HELP IN DISPOSING OF A BODY? and the by now familiar telephone number.

The implications of the new note did nothing to allay his fear. Was he being followed, watched?

It occurred to him that even though Meg had been killed and left in his hotel room, he had an alibi: he had been with Helen throughout the night. Surely, she would be able to vouch for him and the fact he had been nowhere near the hotel at the time of Meg's death. If he were to be hauled in by the police, she could confirm the fact.

Should he therefore turn himself in and take the risk?

He was sitting on a bench in Central Park, looking ahead at the Armory building. The yellow cab had dropped him by the Plaza Hotel and he had walked his way here, his suitcase in tow, his mind still in a state of utter turmoil.

Just an Englishman in New York.

4
The Uselessness of Anger

He couldn't think of another place to leave his suitcase and made his way to the Port Authority Terminal. It felt like going full circle.

Locker key in pocket, he hailed a cab and asked to be taken to Delancey Street, where he was hoping Helen might still be in, waiting for him. All the way there the driver kept on listening to abominable rap music, which Leonard, in his current state of anxiety, took a strong exception to.

As the car drove up to the building where he had spent the previous night, he caught sight of a young woman wearing a washed out denim jacket and similarly distressed jeans, dragging a rucksack behind her, walking up the four stone steps to the door. He handed the driver a ten buck note and exited the cab. The young woman, short, cropped hair and wispy-fringed, was digging through her open rucksack, visibly seeking out her keys.

By the side of the door was a line of buzzers, each with a handwritten name to their right. He realised he didn't know the name of Helen's flatmate. Just as the girl was, with a sigh of relief, about to insert her key in the door, Leonard realised how timely her arrival was, and asked her: 'I have to see someone on the 2nd floor, but I don't know the name of the friend she is living with. Can you help?'

She looked up at him, surprised, her lips curling in apparent disbelief.

'I'm on the 2nd floor. The only other apartment there has been empty for several weeks since the old lady who lived there died.'

'Good. I don't mean about your neighbour dying, of

course. You must be Helen's friend. She said you'd gone away for a few days to visit relatives in … I think it was Cedar Rapids, no?'

A puzzled look swept across her face and she took a step back from him.

'What friend? I don't know anyone called Helen …'

'But …'

'I live alone. Have done ever since I moved in here.'

He was reduced to silence

He wanted to ask her if she was sure, but he sensed it would be of no use. Sensibly refrained from pointing out he knew what her apartment looked like, the colour of the curtains, the weak pressure of the shower, that there were posters of The Ramones and Richard Hell on the bedroom wall, that he had fucked someone in her very bed just hours previously. She wouldn't believe him and, worse, might call the police.

He pretended to have confused the building with another nearby one and arranged for a polite retreat, apologizing profusely in the process.

She closed the building door behind her, not without giving him a final, worried glance.

Pensive, he slowly walked north to Washington Square Park where he sat on a bench, watching the resident squirrels dashing around and climbing the trees, and the chess players by the south west corner silently studying the boards and each other.

How had Helen known how the young woman's apartment was momentarily empty, broken in with no sense of effraction and pretended it was where she lived?

Where did she actually live?

And why had she lied to him?

He would go to the Continental Ballroom that night and confront her. No! She had said that tonight was her day off. Or was that just another lie? Tomorrow then.

In the meantime, he had to find a roof over his head for the next few days as he had no wish to return to his hotel, irrespective of the body that might or might not still be in his room. Neither had he any intention of sleeping rough.

It took him ages to hunt down a suitable Airbnb lodging and it was only with reluctance he had to use one of his credit cards to secure it. It was situated in a building on East Houston, within close distance of the Angelika Film Theatre, once a regular haunt of his on New York sojourns, so he knew the area well.

He retrieved his suitcase from the Port Authority locker and settled in. By now, the city had gone dark and it would soon be time to visit the Continental. He felt an actual sense of relief not being in a hotel room any longer; it meant he could cook some meals for himself and not have to rely on fast food outlets or restaurants. He always felt uncomfortable sitting eating on his own, as if it underlined his status as a man of loneliness. There was a supermarket on the corner of La Guardia Place and Bleecker and he stocked up on enough provisions for a few days and back at the studio apartment that he now could call home rustled up a spinach leaf salad, with slices of avocado, olives, artichoke hearts, roast garlic and a ready-made blue cheese sauce. He hastily wolfed up the improvised salad to the very last leaf in a hurry to be at the ballroom by the time the taxi dancers made their communal way to the floor.

While he was eating he switched on the TV set the studio apartment came with and surfed the news channels. There was no mention of a murdered woman found in Times Square hotel. Yet.

It was a busy evening and the mass of male punters were crowding around the dance floor, clutching their tickets, nervously glancing with a sense of quiet desperation at the magic curtains through which the girls would emerge.

If Helen was truly on her night off, she would be missing out on a lucrative few hours of work.

The band began playing a paso doble.

The line of taxi girls swept through the curtain and made their way to the spotlight. Leonard quickly realised Helen was absent.

He waited for a half hour, in case she arrived late, as sometimes happened with the occasional dancer, but by the sixth or seventh dance, the floor now crowded with deft movement and activity, she had not made an appearance.

So, it was indeed her day off.

No worry.

He would certainly return the following night.

He had no choice in the matter.

He required answers and was not planning on going anywhere until he had some.

Now how to kill the time until then? Another 23 hours to go at least, Leonard reckoned. Controlling his impatience, holding back the underlying fear. And, he resolved, not calling that damn telephone number which he had since, much to his dismay, memorized.

Unless.

The Continental Band had just massacred 'Rhapsody in Blue' and what remained of George Gershwin must be squirming in his coffin.

On the floor, the dancers were circling with brio, let loose, like stars crossing the night sky in accelerated motion, smiles fixed at attention, each and every taxi dancer present paired off with partners or possible suitors in hopeful harmony.

But, again, Helen was not part of the dancing contingent,

Maybe he should have expected this? Her disappearing altogether. When one thing went wrong, everything else did. Sod's law.

He helped himself to yet another drink and waited for the evening to conclude. It was a long wait, the band visibly running out of steam, the dancers of energy and the lonely men of hope as one by one the pretty dancers eventually retired past the curtain with a marked weariness in their step, no doubt to clean up and change into their civilian garb and return to their civilian life.

He knew they wouldn't linger in the dressing room and made sure he was outside the Continental's portal before they began their exodus.

He wasn't the only man to linger around.

The first dancer to leave was a tall, coloured woman whose outfit had been glittery in the extreme, constantly catching the beams from the roaming spotlights. Now she was more prosaically just wearing a black T-shirt and pink slacks with a pair of old, scuffed loafers.

'Hi,' he tried to catch her attention.

She disdainfully looked over at him, no doubt accustomed to being accosted by a punter on her exit.

'You didn't dance with me,' she said, reproachfully. 'I would know you if you had.'

'No, I didn't,' he admitted.

'So, what do you want? I'm in a hurry to get back to my kids.'

'There's a girl who's been working the dance floor with you for the past week. Helen. Young. Auburn hair. I presume you know her, working together and all that?'

'Helen?' she stroked her chin as if thinking hard. 'No, I don't.'

'Maybe not personally, but you'll have noticed her, I'm sure. Was she friendly with any of the other dancers?'

'Never seen her. Hey, by the way, you sound English. Are you?'

'I am. I know her away from the Continental, and lost touch ... So just enquiring,' he pointed out. 'She told me she worked here.'

'I haven't a clue who she might be. Really don't. I have to go now, sorry,' she moved away.

He caught up with the next departing taxi dancer, a diminutive Oriental-looking girl whom he had often witnessed on the dance floor gently leading her partners and kindly correcting their mistakes.

Neither had she any clue as to who Helen was and had no memory of her working shifts at the Continental.

Leonard was feeling a sense of panic take a hold of him.

The next three women who stopped to talk to him were all similarly puzzled by his request, not recognising Helen as any co-worker they could recall.

Had he not been on that dance floor with her for hours, he would have believed them. It hadn't been a dream. He still remembered with fond nostalgia the scent of the perfume she used.

But all insisted there was no such person. Neither the name, nor the description rang a bell with the other dancers.

As if she had never existed.

Was she a ghost his feverish imagination had conjured out of his overbearing sense of loneliness? A phantom dancer?

It made no sense.

Why was he the only one who believed in her existence?

He felt as if he was the hapless protagonist in a movie or a book someone else was in the process of improvising behind his back, pulling invisible strings, cruelly laughing as his puppet floundered and began to question his own sanity.

He supposed he could return to the Continental the following day and somehow contact the management, then ask to see their employment records. But it was unlikely they would cooperate and, anyway, he already guessed it would inevitably draw a blank.

Was it all some unholy conspiracy?

Or a dream?

Now Leonard was angry. He knew he was not mad. He had not imagined her. No fucking way.

From the Port Authority to Delancey Street to the Continental Ballroom. Some memories just can't be erased with the bat of an eyelid.

Why was he here? In New York? And why had he found himself on that beach south of Barcelona?

If he was honest with himself, he was running away from reality. Or grief; or guilt.

The grief of losing his wife to a dreadful illness.

The guilt caused by the burning knowledge of his many infidelities and the certainty, now evident much too late, that he hadn't loved her enough.

Lust, opportunities, chance had all conspired to turn him into the bad man he had become and he knew he had long passed the stage where some form of redemption was still on the cards.

But he was a coward and was still sticking around, bamboozled by romantic notions he had picked up from books and the deceitful influence of movies along the way of life.

And an imposter.

So, on the spur of the moment, he had killed a man in Sitges, but hadn't he already been on the path to personal damnation long before?

Deep down, he'd never liked himself, nor enjoyed the face he saw daily in the bathroom mirror.

So, what now, he pondered, that nagging 10-digit telephone number hovering on the brink of his current thoughts?

Locate the elusive if possibly treacherous Helen? Phone whoever was pulling the strings and might be behind his current predicament? Flee the country, but for where? Or none of the above.

He waited a few days, barely leaving his Airbnb refuge, aside from fetching drinks and fruit from the La Guardia and Bleecker supermarket. Watched too much TV, although had you asked him what he had actually seen, he would have been lost for words; in one eye and out the other.

He was briefly tempted to visit the Port Authority Terminal uptown or the Continental again, but couldn't summon the energy to do either.

His nights were full of dreams verging on nightmares, the faces and bodies of women he had known and others he had conjured up from the warped recessed of his imagination or clips he had once watched on porn sites. All of them were silent, but the weight of their glare as they looked down upon him as he fidgeted endlessly between the sheets, was reproachful, even judgmental and made him feel awful, like a guilty man in the witness box being confronted with the undeniable evidence of his misdeeds.

Middle of the night. 3 a.m. That time when the weight of the world feels unbearable. He woke from yet another dream in which he was running through Manhattan streets, dragging his heavy suitcase behind him, its wheels rattling, in a state of utter panic, knowing it contained the body of a dead woman, and he kept on returning over and over to his departure point, going round in circles again and again, his breath failing him, the weight of life increasingly heavy on his shoulders, as he found himself unable to break the surface of the nightmare in which he was imprisoned. In a rare moment of lucidity, he could see all the way through the incriminating suitcase's thin walls and with his newly acquired X-ray eyes watch the dead girl's eyes gazing back at him. Meg. Helen. His wife. Others. All accusatory and damning.

With one final, major effort he managed through sheer willpower to break through the suffocating envelope of the dream and opened his eyes, found his bearings and recognised the walls, windows and contours of the Airbnb studio and breathed a sigh of relief, inhaling with the desperation of a deep-sea diver breaking to the surface after a lengthy immersion.

Leonard took a sip from the large bottle of lemonade he kept on the bedside table. His throat felt raw, dry. Waited patiently for the world around him to regain its normality again. He blinked. It was still night. He glanced at his watch, realised what time it was and knew instinctively he wouldn't manage to find the solace of sleep again tonight, however physically tired and mentally exhausted he was.

He switched the light on.

Reached for the phone.

And dialled the number he had memorised, not expecting it to be manned at this unholy time of night.

It was.

This time it was a woman who picked up. She sounded middle-aged, well-spoken, calm and collected as if being called at such an hour was all in a day's work.

'Yes?'

He held his breath.

'I know it's you,' she said calmly.

'Me?'

'You, Leonard.'

Of course. The puppet master, or was it now a mistress, pulling his strings, denying him the illusion of agency.

He was briefly tempted to slam the phone down on her but knew it would do no good. They would wait for him to call again, or now they knew the number he was phoning from, would deny him the illusion of control.

'Who are you?' he asked.

'The Bureau.'

'And do you personally have a name?'

He hadn't expected her to answer.

'You can call me Ramona.'

'Hello, Ramona. Late to be up, no?'

'You are, aren't you?'

'*Touché* ...'

'I'm glad you finally called ...'

'Did you have Meg killed?'

'Meg? Is that what she called herself?'

Leonard felt a new pit of depression take root in the pit of his stomach. He'd never entertained the thought that Meg had probably not given him her real name. Had she been playing with him all along? Now he would never know who she truly was. His anger simmered.

'Was it really necessary to have her killed to trap me, incriminate me so I would collaborate with whatever nefarious scheme you have in mind?' he asked Ramona.

'She made a bad mistake. The Bureau does not tolerate

such mishaps. And it served a purpose: we're talking now, no?'

'Is her body still rotting away in my hotel room?' There still hadn't been any reports of her being found on the news or online.

'No. The matter has been discreetly seen to.'

He felt some relief hearing this, but also a measure of sadness and anger at the thought of her remains being disposed of in no doubt some undignified manner he didn't wish to speculate about.

He had truly liked her a lot in the short time he had known her. Not trusted her, but the pull of attraction made it so much easier to overcome reservations. He had always been attracted to fire and managed not to get burned too often.

It briefly occurred to him that with Meg's body now metaphorically swept under the carpet, although the reality of her execution remained a brutal fact of life, an unforgivable one at that, he might not now be on the authorities' radar. But the relief was transient. Leonard realised they had their hooks in him now. The Bureau.

The man he was ordered to meet looked like an accountant. Three-piece well-tailored striped suit, polished brogues, dark red necktie, pale complexion and the thinnest of lips from which all trace of colour had been erased. To Leonard he looked like a horror movie ghoul. He had been asked to meet the Bureau's representative in the lobby of the Algonquin. Was having to return to West 44th St a test of his nerves?

'I represent the Bureau,' he presented himself, recognizing Leonard as he passed through the swing doors of the fashionable hotel. He was led to the bar.

'Do you have a name?'

'No.'

He ordered coffees and Danish for both of them, not even seeking Leonard's approval.

He was distant and unforthcoming. Leonard took a strong

dislike to him.

'Ramona, your colleague who mans the night line said you would explain what is required of me ...'

'She is not the telephone operator. She runs the Bureau.'

This came as a surprise.

'Oh ... Why am I not meeting her, then?'

'You don't.'

'And if I insisted?'

'It would do you no good.'

'I see. And if I walked away right now.'

'I wouldn't advise it. It would not be to your advantage.'

'Really?' Leonard felt increasingly uneasy in the recognition he was now caught even deeper in a spider's web he was unable to control and matters could only get worse from now onwards. He sipped the last of his coffee.

'We know who you are and what you did in Spain. We have determined you possess a possible talent that could prove useful to the Bureau and wish to call on your services. Morally, we feel you owe us that, after becoming responsible for the loss of one our better operatives.'

'The Albanian thug?'

'No, the woman you knew as Meg.'

'You want me to become a killer for hire, replace her?'

'Indeed. On an exclusive basis.'

'But I've only killed once and it was in self-defence. To protect her, Meg. How does that in any way qualify me?'

'You did so instinctively and precisely.'

How could they know all this?

'Should I be flattered?'

'We've researched you. You meet the right criteria. The operatives we employ must display all the signs of normal people. We are not seeking thugs, psychopaths, serial killers or ex-military personnel. Experience has demonstrated that once you overcome the moral scruple involved, anyone can kill. It's part of human nature. And you fit the model we have devised over the years.'

'The years? How long has the Bureau been in existence?'

'Much longer than you'd ever believe.'

'And, should I go along with your proposal of … employment, I would duly be paid for each kill? But who pays you? Who employs you to commission the deeds and on what basis?'

'Questions, questions … We have no political agenda. We stay above the fray. Governments, agencies, individuals, groups. It varies. But your only link will be with the Bureau and there will be no need to worry about the wider implications. The Bureau stands like a wall between you and the commissioning party. Compartmentalising is the name of the game.'

'How convenient.'

'No, just logical.'

'And if I turn you down, what happens?'

'We release a night vision recording of what took place on Balmins beach.'

'So, both ways I'm fucked?'

A wry smile crossed the nameless accountant's lips.

'Well, you just about avoided suffering that fate on the beach, didn't you? It would be a shame for it to now happen less, how shall I put it, physically …?

'You bastards.'

'Now, now. It's just the way of the world, Leonard or however you prefer to be called.'

'But I have no training in what I'm sure you'd describe as the art of murder. Aren't you afraid I'd mess things up through my lack of experience?'

'Oh, we'd see to that. Assign you an instructor who would teach you the basics. Specific firearms, weapons, methods. We wouldn't think of throwing you to the wolves with no means of self-protection. I'm confident you will prove a quick learner. Gut feeling …'

'You've personally recruited a lot of … killers, have you?'

'Some, but the Bureau makes the job easier for me. Everyone I see has been meticulously profiled before I come onto the scene.'

'And has anyone ever turned you down?'

'That's for me to know only, Leonard, my dear man.'

'And if I mess up, I'm the one who ends up in a hole in the ground or dumped into the sea?'

'Oh, that was unfortunate. A great loss. And waste. She was so talented.'

What a bloody epitaph!

The cadaveric figure leaned over the low table on which their empty coffee cups sat.

'Had Sitges not happened, Leonard, what sort of life could you look forward to? Don't lie to yourself; you had nothing.'

How could they see through him with such clarity?

They had him pinned down, hook, line and sinker.

'Is anything negotiable?'

'No.'

'Where would I have to be based?'

'We would prefer here, in the USA. It doesn't have to be New York; you could settle anywhere.'

'I like New York. But I'm on a tourist visa. Only valid for, I think a few months, and it precludes any form of employment?'

'There would naturally be no such thing as a contract of employment. But the visa presents no problem. We frequently work for government; it can be easily sorted.'

'How convenient.'

The unlikeable man smiled, smugness spreading across his pale features, aware the argument had been won and it was now just a question of sorting out the details.

Leonard still had a hundred questions. But only one mattered.

'What about the taxi dancer? She said she was called Helen.'

'Nothing to do with us,' he was informed.

Was the man lying? And, if so, why?

'Where is she?'

'I have no idea.'

Leonard sighed. The net around him had closed. What was

the point of struggling?

'Where do I sign on the dotted line?' he asked.

'There will be nothing in writing of course. Your word suffices, no need for formalities.'

Leonard nodded.

'Welcome aboard.'

A week later in a diner on the outskirts of Brooklyn, Leonard met up with Hopley.

5
Hopley's Waltz

There was a well of contradictions inside Hopley. It was visible to the naked eye. He had long accepted its existence and never tried to fight it or complain. It was just a part of him, a silent one, an entrenched characteristic that did not invite sympathy or pity. It was just what made Hopley something of a cipher to strangers and not the sort of person who made friends. He navigated through life, content with his lot, his only compass the satisfaction of being a good killer. A consummate professional.

What made him good at his job was the fact that he blended in with whatever environment he was travelling through, unremarkable in appearance or the way he dressed, never betraying what he was thinking, almost nonchalant, seldom raising his voice unnecessarily, a chameleon of a man. He was polite to strangers but remote, attentive to detail but easy-going. You could even say he was born to the part, having projected a similar aura of outward indifference since his childhood, although he had not completed his first kill until his late 20s.

He enjoyed the company of women, played the game of desire with elegance and they liked him too, although at some point the more sensitive amongst them would realise there was a core of unattainability within him and they would not so much tire of him, but conclude there was something lodged deep in his soul that didn't respond fully to sentimentality and all that Hallmark jazz. Women and Hopley would always part on good terms, the former with good thoughts tinged with regret in their heart, the latter resigned to the familiar pattern of affection briefly shared followed by inevitable abandon.

He'd been working for the Bureau for several years and helped induct a couple of newcomers, so when asked to explain the ways of death to Leonard, he welcomed the prospect of a few weeks away from the killing fields. He was never assigned more than a couple of hits a year but somehow targets over the past 30 or so months had all involved travel away from New York and he was glad to have a break from airports, and the often complicated arrangements to procure certain weapons locally, all too often involving strangers he couldn't always trust. He was a lone wolf, always worked alone and disliked having to rely on external help.

He selected the place to meet: a diner in Gravesend, a corner of Brooklyn he had often driven by but never eaten in before.

To any outside observer they would just be two random strangers. The Bureau had not given him a name; just mentioned the guy was English, new to the trade and suggested he teach him the basic ropes.

'I don't want to know your name and I won't tell you mine. We've a week or so to go over stuff, and then we'll never see each other again.'

'That's fine by me.'

Two unremarkable men in late middle-age sharing breakfast in a busy diner where the smells of coffee and bacon wafted around while the waitresses addressed the regulars in a mixture of Italian and English and called you 'Honey' even if they hadn't met you before.

Leonard felt as if they were characters in an Edward Hopper painting, anonymous, ordinary.

But what struck him most was the fact that there was something deeply familiar in his interlocutor. As their meeting continued, he began to realise how much they had in common, not just their age but a certain lassitude, an acceptance of the roads that had led them here. The man facing him across the table, dark brown eyes, salt and pepper hair, buttoned-down blue Oxford shirt, did not look like a killer. But then, neither did he.

'If you can avoid the use of weapons, then always do so. It's cleaner. Make it look as if their demise is just an accident. Falling out of a window has a low rate of survival. Being pushed into incoming traffic, likewise. It's far from elegant and you have to be wary of CCTV cameras. Always scout the area or the nearby buildings accordingly. It's all in the small details, the factor that might keep you out of trouble after the act. But death by accident is always good; doesn't arouse suspicion or attract police involvement.'

Leonard nodded, making internal notes. The breakfast shift in the diner was in full swing, the noise, coffee machines, conversations, the large screen TV in one corner all competing to form a hubbub of distraction and making the possibility of anyone overhearing them unlikely.

'Try and always look anonymous. No bright colours in your clothing, rings, jewellery, anything out of the ordinary that onlookers or passers-by might recall if questioned. You have to be an everyman ...'

'What about my voice? There is no way I can fake an American accent ... Surely, that would be remembered.'

'Just keep your mouth shut. Don't ask questions. Do your research before you set foot in the area in which you plan to be active.'

'Research ...'

'Yes. Research, research, research. Everything is in the planning. I've always found it's 90% planning and 10% action. Treat it like a job.'

'You make it sound easy.'

'It's not but you have to think that way; believe in yourself and your ability to complete the task.'

'And when things go askew?'

Leonard remembered the beach and the moment his world had gone topsy-turvy.

'Then you have to rely on instinct.'

'Instinct?'

Hopley suggested they move on. He left a ten dollar note on the table and they walked out of the diner.

Later, cruising down the boardwalk in a wintery Coney Island, the conversation moved on to weapons.

'I'll take you to a firing range later in the week and we'll see what your aim is like and I might be able to correct things like stance and all that. I'll also advise on the type to opt for, depending on your aptitude ...'

'I've never owned any guns,' Leonard pointed out.

'I wouldn't expect you to. Neither do I.'

'So?'

'The Bureau will procure the right weaponry and ways to get it into your hands. But you will have to specify what your precise requirements might be.'

'Which I won't know until I've completed my research?'

'Exactly.'

They stood watching the Atlantic waters lap the shore, wavelets breaking in metronomic rhythm against the wooden stanchions holding up the boardwalk.

'Do you ever use knives?'

'I personally dislike them. They require the approach range to your target to be closer than is safe, and some people have experience with close combat, from bar fights, military training and such. I wouldn't recommend using one. I have never done so. I'd only do so if it was a last resort. But then we all have preferences.'

The image of Meg's body came to his mind out of the blue.

'Have you ever used piano wire?'

Surely it couldn't have been this mild-mannered man by his side who had done the deed.

'No. That's medieval and a terribly cruel way to kill. Messy too. And would take ages for the victim to die. We're not butchers, you know. A good job is a clean job. I never would ...'

'It was just a thought ...' Leonard felt relief.

Hopley changed the subject, possibly sensing Leonard's fleeting sense of discomfort.

'When it comes to your target, the Bureau will with every assignment present you with a dossier about the target:

location, routines, quirks, protection if any, repetitive habits, vehicles owned, immediate travel plans if known, etc ... All this information will have been collected by reliable freelance operatives who then have no further involvement. Naturally, you will have to memorise all the data before disposing of it safely, with no exception. They are very exacting on this point.'

'Quite understandably so.'

Leonard was intensely curious about this man facing him and was terribly curious right then to ask him how many people he had killed but refrained from doing so. The ghoulish Bureau representative had already informed him after he had agreed to inevitably come aboard, how much he would be paid by hit. The amount was staggering. Not that it was a major incentive. He had attempted a joke and asked if it was tax-free but his dour interlocutor hadn't even sketched the shadow of a smile and had merely pointed out that they could assist in opening a Swiss bank account or with a financial institution in the Cayman or British Virgin Islands if he so wished.

Hopley and he agreed to meet again the following morning in Central Park where Hopley would try and instruct him in the art of surveillance, how to follow someone without being spotted.

Later in the week, they would make arrangements to journey to upstate New York for some weapon training and shooting practice, although Hopley was insistent they travel separately as part and parcel of the ritual he was in the process of teaching Leonard.

And then he waited.

He had been paid half in advance for the first job and arranged a six-month rental on Wooster Street in SoHo from an academic who was going to be away for several years lecturing at the Sorbonne, after being offered tenure there. Thanks to the Bureau's services, his references were impeccable, and he now had a permanent visa stamp in his passport, conditional on him not taking up any employment. Killing for hire, he reckoned, did not form part of that remit.

The view from his bedroom window faced a brick wall just a few meters away, and the front of the loft overlooked Wooster and a large factory outlet store advertising massive discounts on different major brands every fortnight in turn.

He fell into a peaceful routine, wandering the Manhattan streets, exploring parts of the city he didn't know well, catching movies at early performances again where he could enjoy the freedom of vast auditoriums as if it was almost a private screening.

On too many occasions, he was tempted to revisit the Continental or Delancey Street, but refrained from doing so, aware it would awaken his anxiety and although he had only known the young woman who called herself Helen so briefly, she had touched his heart in a strange way and he felt the sorrow of losing her profoundly, a situation he found unsettling and that he was unaccustomed to.

On a yellow post-it note he kept in his wallet he had written down three telephone numbers the Bureau had provided him with and asked to memorise. In the febrile state of mind that was now his constant, he was afraid he wouldn't remember them accurately and had taken the risk of scribbling them down until he was confident he could imprint them in his memory. Each preceded by a letter. E for Emergency; W for Weapons and D for Body Disposal. It had been emphasised the final one was to be avoided if possible and only used as a last resort.

All other contact with the Bureau would be one-way only: assignments, instructions, even travel arrangements when required would be made for him, no doubt to muddy waters, mask where the funds used to book planes or hotels originated. The operation seemed slick and professional; Leonard just hoped he could satisfy their exacting demands.

Initially, once a fortnight or so, his landlord, the lecturer, would call him front his French capital to check whether any urgent messages had been left for him on the loft's phone and asked him, on occasion, to open any mail received that appeared important.

While he spoke to him, Leonard could sometimes hear in the background the sounds of Paris. Every city has a particular voice and he remembered Paris well. He had studied there in the often-lonely years preceding his marriage and the place still held a torrent of bittersweet memories. Manhattan was another kind of music altogether.

Guilt is insidious. He could recall the name of every single woman he had dated in Paris, decades ago, but now found it difficult to visualise with any precision his wife's features when they had been younger and happy, or at any rate relatively so. Each thought of her now just dredged up the face of an old woman, her skin pulled tight, her white hair pulled back, non-verbal now, babbling like a child on a hospital bed, hunting for words, her mind in shreds, staring at him with undiluted horror in her eyes, not recognising him, but the eyes, oh the eyes piercing through his soul full of reproach and anger, accusing him, hating him, damning him to walk the roads of hell forever and after.

He was sufficiently aware that he was seeking punishment not redemption, although he also realised having agreed, albeit under duress, to become a killer for hire was a curious way of doing so, but his mind was stretched over too many dimensions of bleakness to accept the irony of his situation.

He had always walked a lot in Paris, the trek over the rue Saint Denis towards the Place du Chatelet and then the crossing of the river before reaching Place Saint Michel and the Latin Quarter an immutable ritual. Two worlds: the ageing and heavily made-up prostitutes lurking in the darkened doorways of rue Saint Denis (where he had actually lived as rents were then cheap there) in contrast with the fresh-faced and short-skirted younger students and foreign tourists swarming across the 6th arrondissement.

It was like a dam bursting and memories flooding back.

Holding Nicole's hand as they crossed the road by Notre-

Dame cathedral. Years later, an affair that didn't happen, Sofia coming up to his hotel room, sitting on the narrow bed, her knee touching his, looking something up onscreen, her scent overpowering and Leonard fighting the impulse to touch her indecently. Maryann stretched out naked on his bed in the St Denis apartment, telling him he could freely do anything to her but for god's sake not to touch her breasts. Him loitering outside the window of Lois's hotel room, hoping for a glimpse of her; their walk back from the party where they had met, following the path of the river all the way from the 16th arrondissement … Paris a patchwork of women.

He even used to have a favourite bar there on the rue St André des Arts, run by a skinny woman from the Auvergne who didn't mind impecunious students taking hours to finish a single espresso and flooding the poorly-lit establishment at all hours, no doubt scaring off better financially-endowed potential customers. A decade later she would sell the place and retire, and it had sadly become a kebab joint.

The thoughts of Paris past made him smile as he put the phone down on his landlord and the echoes of Paris faded. Maybe he should find a similar, welcoming haunt here in Manhattan? Somewhere he could waste time without glancing at his wristwatch, linger, people watch, relax?

It came to him that he already knew the perfect place. Wanda's Café. How had he not remembered it?

He slipped his leather jacket on, picked up a scarf and left the loft apartment, heading to Houston and walking unhurriedly West until he reached Tribeca where he swerved and made his way to the Meatpacking District.

He walked into the café and the owner greeted him effusively as if he was one her regulars. 'Ah, the quiet English guy who seldom smiles is back …'

Yet again it felt to him as if he was passing through a time portal to an older, less frantic era. The customers spread around the dozen or so tables nursing coffees and pastries all in the same mould, comfortable in their own skin, unaffected by the pressures of the outside world.

But the woman with the baby and the pram was nowhere to be seen. Her name, he recalled, was Georgia. She was the one whose presence didn't quite fit, like a refugee from reality seeking shelter in a safe haven. He'd already had a large cup of coffee earlier today and there was a limit to the amount of caffeine he could take on so quickly in succession, so he ordered a Coke. 'No ice, please.'

He was aware Coke also contained caffeine but had long convinced himself that it had a lesser impact in that form and wouldn't keep him awake more than he already did at night, a regular subscriber to insomnia, and even more so since the beach at Sitges and its dire consequences.

'We only serve Pepsi,' she noted.

'Fine with me. I'll live dangerously.'

'Live now, pay later,' she retorted, chortling away as she stepped back to her countertop to fetch his soda. It came in a bottle, not a can, which as far as he was concerned gave Wanda's Café extra brownie points.

Someone had abandoned an old tabloid newspaper on the next table and Leonard picked it up and browsed through it. No bodies in hotel rooms or strangled women washing up on the Jersey shore.

An hour flew by. His soda lost its fizz.

He became familiar with the regulars.

He became a fixture too at Wanda's Café.

The owner who had succeeded the original Wanda was actually called Trisha and hailed from Vancouver. Accents were not Leonard's forte and he hadn't initially realised she was Canadian. She worked throughout the day, with just another local waitress hired to help out from breakfast to the lunch hour and two quasi-invisible cooks manning the kitchen and the cleaning up behind the swing door that led to the kitchen. She lived in an apartment above the café. Her warm, welcoming temperament acted as a shield, as she always deflected any questions about her past life but did so without offending or showing any form of irritation. She valued her privacy but was also a talented inquisitor and knew the back stories of almost all her regulars.

The stories they told!

There was Keith, the bad boy, who had done jail time for assault. And Kris the ex-cop who had fallen from grace but still stood ramrod straight when he spoke to you and displayed a soft kind of elegance, narrow-eyed, bearded, the boom of his bass-profundo voice soothing. Mumbling in his corner was the crazy one, an elegant old man who invariably wore a white three-piece suit that had seen better days and affirmed he had once been a famous magician. One who could make women disappear. When someone, irritated by his posturing, would query his past exploits and challenge him to disappear them, the magician would complain that he only disappeared young women and certainly not men of an advancing age! Every room needed a crazy soul.

Many of the regulars were pensioners who made it their mission to complain how the city had changed in their lifetime and things were not what they were. They eked our their coffees and Danish to make them last and time slow down, and Trisha was generous in allowing them to accumulate small tabs in the week before their welfare or retirement checks landed.

Over lunch, the café transformed into a small-time diner although the menu was very limited: meatloaf, creamy chowder, thick pastrami sandwiches bursting at the seam, bowls of steaming pasta drowning in tomato and onion sauce. The food would never earn a Michelin star but it was filling and full of flavour.

The midday crowd was different if of necessity transient: local office and store workers, traffic wardens and cops, young secretaries for insurance companies and freight companies having swapped their high heel pumps for trainers to give their feet some relief from their mandatory work attire.

Then, on the stroke of two, the intruders would melt away back to their day jobs leaving the place to the regulars who would resume their comfortable, quiet routines and Trisha would get the opportunity to rest for an hour or so behind the countertop, catching her breath, massaging her swollen ankles and toting up the takings.

'So what happened to Georgia, the girl with the baby?'

'It's a long story ...'

'I like long stories.'

'I think it's her story to tell, though,' Trisha said. 'I expect her to return. That's been her pattern, I fear, although good for her if she manages to break the cycle.'

Leonard felt the steely gaze of Kris, just a few tables away at the far end of the café, drilling into him.

The following day, he asked Trisha 'What is it about Kris and Georgia? Something I should know?'

'He's soft on her. Wants to protect her. But the gal knows it's dangerous territory; his past, hers; the age difference, the boyfriend out there in the wild she still pines for. Complicated stuff.'

Then, that very afternoon, Georgia did return, pushing the pram ahead of her, her eyes red, brimming with tears. She found a table, dropped wearily into her seat and looked around, her features a palette of abominable sadness.

Trisha walked up to her and with a paper napkin wiped away the girl's tears from her cheek.

'Didn't work out?'

'No,' Georgia sobbed.

'He didn't want you back? Or the baby?'

'It's not that way,' Georgia said, her chest still heaving. 'It was too late. He's enrolled. For two years ...'

'The bloody army?'

'Yes. I never thought he would,' she said.

'He's a fool. He doesn't deserve you or the child.'

'What am I going to do now?'

'You'll be alright, you see. He just wasn't worth it ... There's still some chowder left. I'll get you some. Put some meat on your skinny bones, girl,' Trisha said.

'Can I have some milk for the child?'

'Of course,' Trisha retreated to the kitchen, while Georgia gently extracted the swaddled baby from the pram and the blankets protecting it. The child couldn't have been more than six months old.

Leonard felt he had inadvertently fallen into a story, like Alice in her proverbial hole in the ground, but one where he had failed to read the opening chapters and was now struggling to comprehend the underlying plot. It was a lot to deal with, seeing that his new Manhattan life was also unfolding like a book or a movie, and he felt uneasy juggling two stories at a time.

Best remain an observer, he figured.

He had enough to deal with already.

He melted back into the fuzzy but comfortable environment of Wanda's Café, just another anonymous regular with time to kill, and a bag full of memories.

What with the far from forgotten Helen, did this new-found attraction to younger women mean he was turning into a dirty old man? Surely not, he had always enjoyed the spectacle of them, but of course he had then been younger. How did they all remain so young, each new generation delivering a renewed batch of temptation. Surely he had not changed, and it was the world around him growing older?

The routine became a pleasant one. Restricting himself to a lone cup of coffee a day, a couple of Cokes or lemonades, sometimes a glass of grapefruit juice, a soup or a sandwich at lunch, perusing the daily newspapers and reading a paperback for a few hours. Day, in, day out. Why did he find routine so comforting?

And then, when he had almost given up on the prospect, the call came. He was about to leave the apartment for the café when the phone rang. He knew it wasn't his landlord as they had spoken the previous evening and he had updated him on messages and mail. Which had triggered a not unpleasurable night of dreams of Paris and women past.

There was to be no face-to-face meeting, just a dossier for him to retrieve which would provide all the necessary information. He would find it in a luggage locker at the Port Authority and the key was in his letter box in his building's foyer. It was an unfamiliar male voice conveyancing the information in a flat, disinterested tone.

The location didn't come as a major surprise following on from Meg's costly negligence.

He was given the number of the locker the key would fit.

Once he had read the dossier and arranged for the necessary preliminary reconnaissance, he could if required call on one of the numbers he had initially been given should he require further information or access to a suitable item of weaponry.

His interlocutor didn't allow him time for any questions and curtly hung up on him.

Leonard took a deep breath, now conscious he was in at the deep end but determined to take matters one step at a time, prove patient and organised.

He retrieved the dossier on the target, dropped it into the Strand Bookstore tote bag he had brought along without even so much as a glance at it. Just a cheap plastic folder, stuffed with a dozen A4 sheets of paper. As instructed he left the small key to the exiguous locker in its lock, indicating it was now empty and available for use again. He noted it was a different luggage locker to the one he had hunted down following the Sitges fiasco. Made sense to use different lockers and not always the same one.

Back on Wooster Street, he finally pulled the pages out, sprawled on the sofa and began perusing them.

His heart dropped all the way down to his stomach when the first sheet of paper revealed a black and white passport-issue photograph of a woman, late middle-aged, peroxide blonde, narrow eyes and thin lips. Her features appeared tanned, against the obligatory white background she was posed against. Possibly Latina.

Leonard paused.

Somehow he had never given any thought to the possibility that the first person he would be assigned to eliminate would be a woman.

His mind rebelled against the prospect.

He dropped the page to the floor as he collected himself, losing all interest in the remaining sheets comprising the dossier.

The shock was profound.

How could he have not even thought of this possibility?

But then again he was well aware that the Bureau was not testing him. He was the one at fault, some reluctant zone in his brain never having remotely considered that the target might be a woman. In books and movies, weren't most of the bad guys always men?

With a rising sense of dread, he remembered that unforgettable vision of Meg's dead, naked body on display, laid out like a macabre work of art.

Women die too.

He thought back to what his instructor had said at the firing range, 'Think of them as targets, not individual persons. It's just a job, and you might as well do it well or at least competently.'

Easy to say, the guy had probably killed a score in his career. Women, too, he now realised.

For an hour or so Leonard tried to ignore the dilemma but then could no longer stand his tangled procrastination.

He had visualised the Bureau contact numbers.

But which to call? None actually seemed appropriate to the situation he found himself in.

He dialled the emergency one.

It rang a half dozen times before it was picked up. There was an echoey sound to the line; he assumed it was scrambled and safe.

'My dear Leonard. To what do we owe the honour?'

It was the woman who had taken his first call. Who had called herself Ramona. Surely it wasn't her real name?

'I've picked up the dossier.'

'I know.'

'The ... person you want me to deal with is a woman.'

'Indeed she is.'

'I wasn't expecting it to be ... I find the fact disturbing.'

'You shouldn't.'

'Well ...' She interrupted him.

'Do you think every assignment will be a Lex Luthor or some monstrous fiend straight from the comic books? If only it were so easy.'

He nodded his understanding although she couldn't see him.

'I know, but ...'

'No buts, Leonard. The Bureau has entered into a contract and it falls to you to deliver. I am aware it will be your first time. Technically speaking Sitges doesn't count as it was a spur of the moment thing. I'll do you a favour then, Leonard. I will not be in a position to do so again in the future, but right now I'm sympathetic to your plight. I can inform you that this woman IS an evil person. She is responsible for the spread of deadly drugs and is heavily involved in human trafficking. Of women, of minors. She deserves no sympathy. Does knowing that help a little?'

'I suppose so,' he said.

'Good. So repress those qualms of yours, Leonard, and demonstrate you have what it takes. I know you can do it.'

'Nice to know you believe in me when I'm unsure myself.'

'Gut feeling. We chose you. It wasn't an easy decision.'

'OK.'

'Now, there is no hurry. Take your time, study the dossier we have provided. Do some preliminary surveillance. Find out her routines, her weaknesses, plan matters in detail. And you'll know when to strike. She is bad. And gender doesn't come into it. Trust me.'

He wouldn't have trusted Ramona if his life depended on it. Even though he had no proof, he was certain she was the person at the Bureau who had sanctioned Meg's death and the disgusting manner in which it had been arranged for him to witness the terrible aftermath, all to drag him deeper into the Bureau's net. No, he might now embark on a killing career for them, but he would never trust the Bureau.

He hung up before he betrayed his feelings further.

He picked up the dossier and stacked the pages on the corner of the sofa and proceeded to slowly read through it, line by line, making mental notes as he went along as the information began suggesting ways and means to approach the woman and isolate her somewhere where the deed could take place.

She lived on the Upper West Side, a career criminal hiding in plain view among the aristocratic moneyed classes of Manhattan.

Her name was Carlotta Valdes.

Amongst her many above the crime line activities and involvements, she was also a part owner of the recently refurbished and re-opened Continental Ballroom.

There was no such thing as coincidence.

6
Let's Do the Continental Shuffle

The first thing Leonard ascertained, on his initial recce, was the fact that Carlotta Valdes lived in a high-rise building not far from the Dakota, and the place had a permanent doorman and likely security so therefore not easy to access without leaving some kind of compromising record.

For a brief moment, he wondered if Carlotta, through her Continental Ballroom connection, was possibly behind Helen's disappearance, but dismissed the idea. It would make no sense. There were no apparent degrees of separation; Helen, the Bureau, Carlotta, him: all he could see was a broken line. No way.

Hopley – although he hadn't actually known his name – had said that no job should be rushed. That you should take the time it needed to do it right, plan and plan again, seeking out the opportunity, the gap between the cracks. He had advised Leonard that it was rare for the Bureau to ever set a specific date or time constraints. They were professional and knew better.

If the place she lived was out of bounds, then he should pinpoint her haunts, the places she visited on a regular basis whether for business or for pleasure, come to understand her routines and therefore her possible weaknesses.

The weather was getting colder as the year grew older. The wind roared from north to south like an apprentice banshee down the Manhattan Avenues, hemmed in, breaking apart at the intersection where the Flatiron Building stood like a ship's prow, both its invisible tongues surging ahead in parallel streams towards the butt end of the island.

He had followed Carlotta from her apartment building to a brief meeting she had with an associate in Washington Square Park by the now empty fountain. The man was also Latino-looking and wore a denim jacket over a black shirt and they appeared from afar to be having a heated conversation. Nothing changed hands that he noticed. Then Carlotta returned uptown to her place while the man exited the park and headed to Broadway. Why had they met here, when Central Park would have been a nearer place for Carlotta to avoid anyone eavesdropping on their conversation?

Leonard took a photo of the man for future reference. Carlotta didn't make it outside for the rest of day, as he took refuge from the increasingly unpleasant weather on a corner across the street, hoping he looked inconspicuous in leather jacket and cargo trousers, with a Penguin Classics tote bag slung across his shoulder, and attentively kept watch on the door to her building.

As darkness fell in late afternoon and the fierce winds abated, he gave up for the day, hoping this wouldn't prove a lasting pattern in which case he was truly fucked.

Patience would be required. A lot of it.

In the flesh, albeit from a safe distance, Carlotta Valdes was not quite the same as the passport photo he had been supplied with. Her peroxide blonde hair was elegantly streaked with grey, and her posture ramrod straight, emphasised by the vertiginous high heels she invariably wore. Her thin lips were coloured bright red, like a deliberate, artful stain painted across her features. Somehow her appearance was more one of a late middle-aged university lecturer than a drug smuggler and human trafficker. Following her had proven easy; she never turned round, backtracked, checked around her or in shop windows and just glided through the city with a form of arrogance. Her posture screamed out 'I own this bloody city'.

The second day of surveillance yielded better results. She took several meetings at which fat envelopes were seen changing hands, after which she would deposit their content in a nearby Chase Bank branch, laundering the cash in full view as if it were a daily occurrence. The men she encountered, in bars, hotel lobbies overlooking Central Park and anonymous diners, varied in age and looks. But all seemed to defer to her, lackeys, sidekicks, soldiers she controlled, reporting back on their activities, delivering tainted offerings harvested from illicit activities.

Slowly a picture was emerging but not, so far, an opening that could bring him into closer contact with her and the opportunity of fulfilling his contract with the Bureau.

He persevered, carefully jotting down the places she visited, the men she encountered, the times, in a small notebook he would have to promptly dispose of once the job had been completed.

The third day tailing Carlotta drew a blank as she never even left her building.

Leonard was tempted to take a day off. His nose was running and his throat sore from all the walking in the cold and waiting at mostly standstill while he observed her encounters from a secure distance. But he overcame his reluctance and was at his post early the following morning and was rewarded by Carlotta leaving her building at an early hour.

He duly followed.

And ended up at the Continental Ballroom.

She was let in through a side door. Naturally at this time of day, the Continental was closed for business and he was in no position to find out who she might be meeting with inside, but assumed it would be in the offices with one of the frontmen running the place.

She didn't emerge until midday and hailed a passing yellow taxi. He was unable to find another vehicle and lost her. He sighed. He could, he knew, travel to her apartment building and wait to see when she arrived home. She was bound to return there but witnessing her arrival would not advance his plans.

That evening he resolved to visit the Continental again.

There was a different band on the elevated stage overlooking the ballroom floor. They mostly played the same standards as their predecessors, although there was more of a swing in their efforts, a sprinkling of jazz, with more regular solos by the trumpet and saxophone players in the brass section. They all wore white tuxedos, with a paper rose in their jacket buttonhole, oiled slicked back hair, looking as if they just arrived here through a time machine from the depth of the 1940s.

Some of the taxi dancers he observed were new, while others who had stood out from the crowd on his past visits were now absent. It wasn't as if it was a job with much in the way of career advancement or prospects, he knew, and hard on the body. But they were all fresh-faced and agile on their feet, smiling with just the right amount of sympathy and come-hither vibes at the gentleman callers willing to pay for a dance. And pay they did, queuing politely, never pushy, waiting in some instances for their favourite dancer to become free and clutching their dance tickets in sweaty palms, with hope eternal in their heart.

Leonard took a stool at the bar, ordered a soda, and when the time felt right entered into a casual conversation with one of the bartenders. She was no older than most of the dancers, had a pronounced Southern twang and rosy cheeks behind the make-up which didn't succeed in hiding the flurry of freckles spreading across her nose and cheeks.

'Does working at the bar pay better than dancing?' he enquired.

She smiled back at him.

'Sadly no,' she said. 'But I found out I ain't no good at dancing. All those steps and styles that were in vogue before I was even born, I was just getting them all mixed up. Nearly fell on my face several times before I had to give up. But the management took pity on me and offered me this here job.'

Looking down at her significant cleavage, Leonard understood why.

'But the tips do help out,' she added, looking him straight

in the eye.

'I'm sure they do,' he moved a green bill to the countertop.

She briefly lowered her eyelids in acknowledgment. They had an understanding; for now.

'So ... they treat you well?'

'Could be worse.'

The band started up 'Mood Indigo'. The dancers on the floor shuffled and regrouped.

'So, is there an actual manager?'

'Yes, that's Patrice.'

'French?'

'Actually not. He's from New Jersey. Straight out of Central Casting, if you ask me ...' she giggled.

'You mean, mob-related?'

'I couldn't say. But none of my business, if you ask me.'

'Duly noted.' So what's your name?'

'Ruby Rose.'

'That's lovely.'

'And you? Do you have a very English name?'

'Not really.'

'So what is it?'

He had a slight hesitation. 'Adam,' he lied, ever aware of the motive behind his enquiries and the need not to leave any possible clues as to his identity.

Her attention was drawn to another customer ready to order at the other end of the bar counter.

'I'll be back,' Ruby Rose called out as she swivelled away.

Later, he asked her about the offices, getting confirmation they were situated upstairs as he had expected. But Ruby Rose didn't have any further information about the running of the Continental that might prove useful to him. His attention was drawn back to the now crowded dance floor which had become a whirlpool of action as the band had increased their tempo and the dancers followed right on cue, puppets moved by the invisible strings of the surging melody, full-sized atoms colliding and repelling each with each beat of the music.

Ruby Rose was now busy as new customers converged

towards the bar. He didn't think he could get much more information from her, anyway.

Maybe time to call it a day?

A lull in the music as the white-tuxedoed musicians paused momentarily and sipped water or more challenging beverages from their hip flasks.

Then, it was their turn to play David Bowie's 'Let's Dance'. Leonard remembered dancing to that song with Helen, and her hand had moved down to his waist and she had looked at him with more than curiosity in mind, inquisitive, dreamy and he had realised they had formed some sort of connection. That was the night he had waited for her outside and they had slept together. In fact, the last night he had seen her before her unexplained disappearance and everyone denying she had ever existed. Aside from him.

He picked up his leather jacket from the coat check and walked out of the Continental. It was well past midnight and the sky was clear of stars. The faint smell of exhaust fumes lingering in the air.

He arrived early the following day outside the Continental, planning to stick around until the necessary deliveries of booze and such would arrive. Surely, the place must have arrangements for such deliveries on a daily basis? They wouldn't be able to operate without a regular supply of goods. Observe who was present to open the door to the drivers. Maybe engage in conversation; find a pretext to get inside during daytime.

His assumption was right. Around ten in the morning, a large delivery van parked outside and its burly, cap-wearing driver walked up the steps and rang the buzzer by the goods entrance.

A minute later, the door opened. A young guy in overalls greeted the delivery guy and let the door ajar for the provisions soon to be unloaded off the van.

Leonard waited for the right occasion when the delivery

guy was busy at the back of the van piling up boxes and cartons of booze and the Continental attendant –a cleaner? – was back somewhere in the bowels of the cavernous building, and swiftly slipped through the unattended door.

There was a warren of corridors, some of which he knew led to the dance floor, the backstage area, the actual entrance foyer and the dancers' changing rooms, which he ignored. At the back, he found the stairs that must lead to the area where the offices must be situated.

He took them one step at a time, trying to think of a plausible excuse if he was caught short wandering around.

Another narrow corridor with two closed doors on either side of its length came into view. Visibly, the first floor, or as memory reminded him what Americans were in the habit of calling the second floor as the ground floor was illogically given a number.

However, this was where his luck ran out, as both doors were locked.

He retreated downstairs.

And came face to face with the attendant, who was piling up the deliveries into a storage space to the left of the bar.

'Who are you?'

Leonard improvised.

'The door was open, so I thought I'd see if Patrice was in.'

'He never comes in until after lunch,' the young guy in overalls said. 'I'm the only one around in the morning. Cleaning up the joint, checking on deliveries. Who are you?'

'Just a businessman ...' he was playing it by ear. 'I know of Patrice. Wanted a chat about a possible financial opportunity. But I haven't his telephone number. Can you help? I'll try and make a formal appointment.'

'I have no idea what his number is. I just take care of things, you know ...'

He could see his presence on the premises was unwelcome and made to leave.

'No problem. The door through there, is it?'

'Yes. Why don't you come back early afternoon. He seldom has meetings then. Just hangs around in his office from what I can see.'

'I'll do that.'

He had time to make a detour to the Meatpacking District and visit Wanda's Café, rather than kill time walking the pavements.

And there it was, a little oasis of old-fashioned comfort, out of time, warm, welcoming, and blessed by the constant presence of Trisha's kind smile and the ever-present sadness in Georgia's eyes. He walked in, bathed in the familiarity of sounds, smells and muted conversations between the regulars staking their territory before the lunch crowd invaded.

He looked around. Kris was not present. He passed Georgia who sat at her usual corner table, munching a Danish and rhythmically moving the baby's pram in a gentle back and forth movement to silently lullaby it to sleep.

'How are you today, Georgia? Getting over things?

'I'm trying,' the young woman said, barely looking up at him, lost in a sea of personal thoughts, 'but it's not easy.'

'Time heals, you'll see,' Leonard said, all too aware that it must sound like a cliché.

Georgia awarded him a faint smile before Trisha finally made an appearance and asked him 'Your usual?'

'Why not?' He sat himself down by a free table,

There were still crumbs of toast scattered across its surface and Trisha promptly brushed them away.

She brought his still fizzing glass of soda. 'Is that all you drink? I thought you English mostly consumed tea.'

'Well, I ain't your average Englishman!'

'Bah, you just want to be different,' she jested.

How different, he hoped she would never find out. The unfaithful Englishman with one murder under his belt and planning another!

A nagging feeling inside him insisted he should go talk to Georgia, a desire to listen to her story, but he knew the time wasn't right. He was no knight errant. That time had come and gone.

He was lying in wait.

A man walked up to the Continental's side door, and Leonard reckoned this could well be Patrice. Dark-haired, skinny, a zigzagging scar across his left cheek, his khaki slacks held up with a gaudy brown leather belt with outsize metal clasps, shiny brand-new trainers and an arrogant air of belonging.

Leonard called out 'Mr Patrice?'

The man turned round and glanced at him.

'Yes?'

He had assumed right.

'Could we talk?'

'About what?'

'Business, of course.'

'What sort of business?'

'The Continental.'

He knew from the dossier on Carlotta Valdes the Bureau had supplied him, that she was a minority shareholder in the ballroom, with around 25% of the equity registered to her name. However, he had no idea who the other investors might be, hidden as they were behind a nest of shelf companies. Instinct taught him that Patrice was just a glorified manager charged by the real owners to supervise the place, but his involvement probably didn't extend any further. It was speculation, but worth acting on. He had rehearsed a possible scenario.

Patrice inquisitively looked him up and down. Leonard looked the part today, in a two-piece suit; actually the only suit he owned here in New York, which he had made to measure on the cheap many years back in Phuket in Thailand. Fortunately, he hadn't gained too much weight since and it still fitted him well.

'So?'

'Might we talk inside. In your office?' Leonard said.

'Are you a cop?'

'Do I look like one? Would a cop speak with a foreign accent?'

'You're Australian?'

Leonard smiled. 'No. English actually.'

'Just kidding.' Visibly Patrice's knowledge didn't extend far beyond the Big Apple and New Jersey.

Pulling a key from his jacket pocket, he inserted it into the door's Yale lock and opened up. Waved Leonard ahead.

Once in the foyer, 'There is just one thing ...'

'Yes?'

'I have to pat you down. I'm sure you'll understand. The Continental is a ... complicated business and my employers, as you probably know well, wish to retain a degree of discretion. Just to make sure you're not wearing a wire or carrying.'

'I fully understand.'

Naturally, Leonard was clean. Patrice's was the office on the left down the narrow upstairs corridor. Patrice sat behind a large desk cluttered with documents. Leonard was shown to a chair facing him across the desk.

'So, what can I do for you, Mr? Do you have a name.'

'Mr George,' Leonard said. 'I represent a group of discreet City of London investors of high wealth. They are interested in acquiring shares in your enterprise.'

'Ah ...'

Patrice scratched his chin, quite unprepared for this.

'Well,' he said, 'I can't really speak for my principals. This is really quite unusual.' He scrutinised Leonard at length. 'Say, have I seen you downstairs before? Weren't you here a few weeks back, dancing with some of the girls? I think I recognise you. Somehow you looked more classy than our normal standard of punter. Was that you?'

Leonard nodded.

'Just doing my homework.'

'I see.' Patrice nodded approvingly. 'Checking us out?'

'Elementary,' Leonard confirmed.

Patrice stood up and indicated a drinks cabinet.

'Can I offer you something?'

'Thanks, but I don't drink.'

'Your loss, Mr George.' He helped himself from a decanter of what looked like whisky.

A thought occurred to Leonard. He hesitated briefly before enquiring.

'You mentioned you'd observed me a while back dancing with one of your ... girls. I actually only danced with one in particular. She said her name was Helen. I was, I must confess, quite taken with her.' He attempted a complicit smile. 'But she appears to have left your employment ...'

Patrice interrupted him. 'The dancers are one area I have no involvement with, I'm afraid. They are in fact recruited by one of our principals. Unfortunately, I'm not even allowed to keep any records concerning them ... My job here is to ensure everything runs smoothly on the logistics and security front.'

'Might it be Mrs Valdes who oversees that specific part of the operation, by any chance?'

'You have certainly done your homework. You're quite correct.'

Leonard felt a buzz in the tip of his fingers. Now to set the bait.

'The investors I represent understand she controls a substantial holding in the company that owns the Continental Ballroom and would be prepared to make a handsome offer for all or part of her share capital.'

Patrice fell silent. He was visibly out of his depth. Again, he scratched his chin with the flat of his hand, probably didn't even realise he was doing it, as he struggled for an answer.

'So why haven't you contacted her direct as you know so much about her and the Continental?' he finally asked.

'Discretion,' Leonard appointed out. 'I would like to meet discreetly, not at a bank or a lawyer's office.'

'Hmm ...'

'Do you have a way of reaching her?' he asked.

'We do have a weekly meeting.'

'Here?' Although Leonard already knew the answer, having followed her to the Continental.

'Yes.'

'Well, might I suggest you allow me to join you on the next occasion she visits, and I can put the proposal to her, away from inquisitive eyes?'

'We meet in this office,' Patrice confirmed. 'But we have other business matters to discuss ...'

'If you could maybe provide us with 15 mins alone, so I might raise the matter at hand? I won't delay your planned meeting any longer than that.' He added, 'I could possibly, subject to a satisfactory outcome, suggest to my clients you could be awarded an introductory fee maybe, some small commission?'

Patrice pondered, weighing the pros and cons.

'And I'd rather you didn't warn Ms Valdes prior to the day. I think she will be more receptive to our offer if it comes out of the blue. No telling her in advance.'

Patrice sat back in his chair, sipped the last dregs of his whisky. Then nodded.

'She will be visiting in two days. She's always punctual. Always gets here at the same time.'

'Perfect. I will arrange to be present ten minutes before. Will that work?'

Patrice agreed.

His scheme had worked. So far.

At close quarters there was something steely about Carlotta Valdes. Not a single hair out of place and a thin smile curled scarlet across her possibly Botoxed features. She was dressed for business in a tailored pinstripe suit more suitable for a Wall Street banker.

They sat in silence in the Continental Ballroom upstairs

office. The way she looked at him was full of disdain. She was angry. At being approached in this manner. He had no doubt that, later, Patrice would bear the brunt of her ire.

'What the fuck do you want?'

Leonard made his pitch.

'This is not uninteresting,' she pointed out, 'if very irregular.'

'I am conscious of that.'

'And also complicated. Yes, it is true I control a significant share of the Continental's assets, but in exchange I also conduct a lot of, should we say confidential business with the company. Between us I can tell you, I am given a high degree of latitude in particular areas of the Continental's activities.'

Was this a reference to the taxi dancers?

Could some of them have been trafficked?

Leonard recalled Helen and the friend who was allegedly putting her up on Delancey Street. Was there some connection there?

He had to think on his feet. Improvise.

'I'm confident my clients would not be averse to retaining existing commercial arrangements, should they acquire your shares, I really do.'

'Now we're talking,' Carlotta said, adjusting the way she was sitting on her chair, no longer defensive.

'Excellent.'

One step at a time.

'So what happens next?'

'Well, now that I am aware of the fact you might be disposed to enter into negotiations, I can report back to my clients and move this one stage further,' Leonard said.

'I'd like that,' Carlotta said. 'I suppose it's premature to enquire at what level your principals might be pitching their initial offer?'

'It is.'

He had her hooked. Greed is a powerful motivation. Maybe the hapless Patrice would not be reprimanded too harshly for letting Leonard into the building and setting the meeting up.

'Good. Just one thing …'

She frowned.

'Yes?'

'Maybe at this stage it would be preferable for you not to give your existing fellow shareholders any hint that we are in negotiation. We'd rather present them with a *fait-accompli* should the two of us agree on the level of compensation.'

'I understand.'

Leonard had speculated that the hit on Carlotta might actually have been commissioned by her other partners, but he kept that to himself.

'I'll need 48 hours, and might I suggest we meet somewhere private for our next round of talks?'

'That's fine with me.'

'Not in public, it goes without saying.'

'We can do so at my apartment.' There was a notepad on Patrice's desk, and she tore off a sheet and wrote down her address with a silver Parker pen she had pulled from her ostentatious Louis Vuitton handbag and passed it over to him.

'Does your building have a doorman? I would prefer my visit to remain completely confidential at this stage.'

Of course he already knew the answer to his question, having lurked round the corner of her apartment block for several days.

'There is a service entrance on 73rd Street,' Carlotta advised him. She snatched the note back and scribbled down four numbers. 'This is the code for the door. I'm on the 11th floor, apartment 1103.'

'That's just perfect, Ms Valdes. Can I have your telephone number. I'll contact you as soon as I have all the elements to take a step forward.' He would have to use a burner if he rang her. Leave no trail of any kind.

It couldn't have worked out better. Best not tempt fate and allow matters to rest here for today. He had kept his patience under control and the ultimate reward now near. His nerves settled.

He stood up and shook her hand. Already he was thinking of a possible scenario unfolding. What sort of weapon would he require? Contacting the Bureau and getting his hands on one. He was nervous at the thought of using a gun. Even with a suppressor. And remembered Hopley's words. That the best possible outcome was to make it look like an accident. Oh well, he thought, it's a long way down from the 11th floor. And hated himself for picturing that outcome. But hadn't Hopley mentioned in passing that it was his own favourite way of disposing of targets, no mess, no suspicions, no cumbersome bodies to get rid of, so convenient ... He had been cynical but also a realist.

In case she had second thoughts and did contact any of other shareholders concerned and leaked the news of the approach, Leonard wasn't planning to wait. He would strike tonight. He had the code for her building's service entrance, which would allow him to bypass any doorman on duty, and planned to make his way to her apartment as soon as possible, and surprise her. The rest he would play by ear.

She opened the door.

There was a look of surprise on her face, her lips curling into a wide O.

'You?'

'Indeed.'

'I wasn't expecting you.'

'I know.'

He had been tempted to take the elevator after rushing stealthily through the lobby while the doorman was taking a comfort break but, eagle-eyed, noticed a camera in the top right corner, so chose to walk up the steps all the way up from the ground floor. It had left him somewhat breathless, but once on the 11th floor he had paused for a while to compose himself, hoping silently that none of the other three doors on this floor would open while he was gathering his strength and his presence was noted.

It was eleven at night and the plush building was a haven of quiet, neither the sound of music, TVs on or voices filtering pass the heavy-set front doors of the respective apartments. Leonard was wearing gloves, careful not to leave prints on any nearby surface. He had bought them for cash from a street seller on Canal Street, right before heading here. They were no doubt counterfeit and not leather, but that did not matter.

She was no longer impersonating the businesswoman she had been earlier in the day in the Continental's office. Her impeccable make-up had been wiped clean off, and she looked ten years older. She wore a satin dressing gown in shades of lilac, cleavage on display, and her hair was still wet. She must have just taken a shower just before he had reached her door, he suspected.

'I wasn't expecting you so soon ...'

'I'm sorry I didn't call to warn you. But I thought you wouldn't mind hearing the news as early as possible.'

'Good news?'

'Absolutely.'

She realised how unkempt she was and, instinctively, pulled the expensive but inadequate for company dressing gown tighter around her waist, although the fact she was probably naked underneath was difficult to disguise.

'So, come on in, Mr George.'

'Thank you.'

'I'd offer you a drink, but I'm afraid you'll have to bear with me while I go and change into something more ... appropriate.'

'There won't be any need. For the drink. Or changing. I won't be staying long. Just sorry I appear to have disturbed you at an inconvenient time. You know how it is in business, you just keep your eye on the deal and become unaware of anything extraneous, like the time of day in my case. As you know London is five hours ahead of New York, so I've had the opportunity to explain the situation to my clients and am pleased to advise they do wish to embark on immediate negotiations.'

'That's wonderful.'

He could smell the fragrance of her shampoo or conditioner, but also the animalistic scent of her nearby body. She was barefoot and surprisingly vulnerable now that she didn't wear heels and her formal business attire. So much smaller than him.

She guided him to a room that served as her office. There was a desk, a safe embedded in the back wall, and a deluge of prints scattered across the perimeter of the room. Or were they lithographs? He recognised work by Warhol, Rauschenberg, Matisse, Ansel Adams, Jack Vettriano, Edward Hopper's 'Automat' which he was familiar with as a variation on it had featured on the cover of a curious thriller he had been reading on the beach in Sitges and had left behind in his haste to quit the Spanish resort and his hotel on the port.

The sofa was a three-seater, its brown leather surface burnished and shiny under the glare of two angle poise lamps set at opposing corners of the room. She pointed to it, and sat at one end, while he did at the other at her request. As she settled into a comfortable position facing him, the lilac robe stretched open over her chest and he had a momentary glimpse of one of the darkest nipples he had ever come across. She quickly realised what had happened and pulled the flaps of the gown back together, although she allowed herself a knowing smile.

A heavy silence fell as both of them waited expectantly for what the other would say next. The heat emanating from her body reached towards him.

He looked away from her, towards the window.

'Do you have a view on the Park?' he asked.

She didn't. He had done his homework. There was another building separating hers from Central Park, similar in architectural style, built in the same period, massive, ornate and, like hers, festooned with small balconies.

'No,' she answered, 'but you can almost see all the way downtown.'

'Must be awesome at night, with all the Manhattan lights

shining bright?'

'It is,' she confirmed. 'Would you like to see?'

'I'd love too,'

She rose, stepped over to the window and opened it. There was a fresh breeze outside that swept into the room. He followed her as she stepped onto the narrow balcony.

She was right: New York was laid out below, like a constellation of white, yellow and random red and blue lights, like a picture postcard.

He took two steps forward to the metal railing where the small balcony ended, looked down. He felt her breath on his neck as she huddled up to him to share the view.

They stood in silence for a moment watching the myriad lights below waltzing in all directions, like a ball captive on the play floor of a pinball machine.

As she leaned over slightly to match his own posture, Leonard abruptly turned towards her and with one hand on her neck, half choking her and causing an immediate state of shock and uncertainty that paralysed Carlotta and left her rooted to the spot, he placed a leg between hers so she could no longer control her balance, and as she struggled for equilibrium and still under the effect of surprise, he seized her by the waist, gave her a forceful push in the middle of the back and Carlotta toppled over the railing and began her fall to the ground below.

Leonard's heart was racing and he imagined the sound of blood coursing through his brain, loud, oppressive, deafening. Then he remembered to breathe.

He didn't look down. Had no need to know how long it took for a body to fly downwards through the air from the eleventh floor to the concrete pavement below.

As the adrenaline ebbed, he was about to turn round and step back into Carlotta Valdes's apartment when he looked up. A lone lit window in the twin building across the street. The silhouette of a woman. Looking straight at him. Had she seen him? Would she be able to describe what he looked like? The questions ran through his mind like a torrent.

He couldn't properly make out her features, just a thin silhouette with long blonde hair to her shoulders, wearing a translucent nightie, through which the shape of her body was clearly contoured. But her face was in darkness.

Damn! A loose end.

He rushed through the empty rooms, closed the door to Carlotta's apartment behind him and rushed down the stairs, checking the doorman had not returned to duty, moved rapidly to the service entrance and found himself on the street.

He made his way into the Park, a zigzagging route away from possible cameras, exited close to the Plaza Hotel and then caught the subway at 57th and rode it all the way to West 4th.

By the time he reached Greenwich Village and was about to cross West Houston, he felt a strange sense of exhilaration, mixed with guilt, and fear.

He had now committed his first proper murder.

He had by now long absolved himself for killing the Albanian on the Spanish beach; had it not been technically self-defence?

7
Through a Dark Window

There was nothing on the next morning TV news about a woman falling to her death on the Upper West Side, let alone any suspicious circumstances surrounding the event.

Like clockwork, though, the rest of the fee agreed by the Bureau landed in a foreign bank account that had been opened in his name.

He'd made crime pay.

He asked himself if he felt any different, but the truth was he didn't in the slightest. He was still the same, supremely imperfect, ridden with guilt for all the petty crimes that had filled his past life, the selfishness, the sin of pride.

But right now, Leonard was worried about the woman whose silhouette he had briefly glimpsed through the backlit window of the upper floor building facing the one Carlotta Valdes had involuntarily taken flight from.

He fed his anxiety with chocolate, although frustrated that American chocolate was just not a patch on British or Swiss varieties and always left a sour, lingering taste at the back of his throat. He could just imagine the headline: KILLER GOES ON CHOCOLATE SPREE!

To calm his nerves, he walked across Houston and watched two foreign movies in a row at the Angelika, if only to kill time. KILLER GOES ON MOVIE SPREE and after leaving the cinema spent an hour idly checking out books from the untidy, dusty shelves and tables at the Mercer Street Bookstore. Ended up with two used paperback copies of old Cornell Woolrich novels he couldn't remember reading, mostly because the atmospheric covers cities at night with neon signs blazing. KILLER GOES ON CRIME BOOK SPREE!

Back at his Wooster Street rental, having picked a Bento box from the nearest bodega, he ate and sat down to read. Now, he recalled having read one of the books ages ago but kept on turning the pages in the impossible hope the desolate heroine's wanderings would this time around reach a different conclusion. And then he fell asleep around midway through the novel. In his dreams, he was rewriting the story but still couldn't prevent the finale from crashing against the rocks of bleakness. Even in dreams, the femme fatale (or the victim) is unable to escape fate.

The death of Carlotta Valdes did make the local news the following day, reported as an instance of a businesswoman with known criminal affiliations committing suicide by leaping from her high-rise window. The way it was reported made it sound as if the case was clear cut and the incident already filed away, with no indication of anything suspicious involved. Traces of drugs and alcohol had been found in her system and might have proven a factor in her decision. Although it was the outcome he had been aiming for, Leonard still harboured a seed of doubt, of loose ends still hanging in the air, with the potential to blow up in his face when he least expected it. A feeling that was unpleasant.

The deed had been committed and he now felt as if he was navigating between two worlds, the before and the after, and the shore either side was increasingly becoming out of reach.

He was alone. But, this time, it felt harder to bear than after having lost his wife.

When that calamity had felled him, he raged against life itself as he came to the realisation that even in the bad periods, he had taken succour from the fact that they had been a couple, and that over the years, despite his introversion, mistakes and many silences, he had no longer been a solitary man but part of something else, something better. In the aftermath he tortured himself by endlessly wondering if he had truly made her happy, damning all the occasions he had not expressed his love for her with sufficient articulacy. That feeling still lingered, alongside the bittersweet memories.

113

True, he had loved others but it had not diminished the power of his love for his wife, even when he had spent time with other women, many of which had plucked a resonant chord in his heart. He'd had too much love to give, share. Now, he had nothing. Just a newly discovered power of life and death over others, at the whim of a shadowy but powerful organisation which had drawn him into its web, pulling invisible strings he hadn't known even existed. He harboured a simmering steam of anger; but anger is exhausting.

Leonard was not a happy man.

But had he ever been?

In one of the old pulp novels he had picked up, a man suffered from amnesia and had no idea what he might have done for the past three years. Leonard was envious. Could this not happen to him?

What now?

Just wait obediently for the next set of instructions from the Bureau? A name, a face, a target and new plans to be made, a step further down a road of no return.

He had experienced the loneliness of widowhood, but the loneliness of the killer he was now mutating into felt even worse.

Winter was on the doorstep, the sky uniformly grey, with clouds like slow-moving hippos nonchalantly stepping across the horizon. The sounds of Manhattan were muted, as if fully expecting to soon be drowned under a blanket of snow, The whole city vibrated with a quiet sense of lassitude.

He roamed the avenues in a dreamlike state, window-shopping, people-watching, or more accurately women-watching, although the heavy coats and shapeless garments most were wrapped in from head to toe spoiled the pleasure, obscuring curves, body shapes, no skin on display let alone the magic arc of ankles in motion.

He had visited New York in the winter before, but had not lived there through a whole season. He wasn't looking forward to it.

He found himself emerging from the Park, the proverbial killer attracted back to the scene of his crime. He could see the building where Carlotta Valdes had lived as it loomed over the neighbourhood, and then quickly glanced over at the opposing high-rise, and looked up, hoping to recognise the window where the possible witness to the defenestration had furtively appeared.

It was difficult to assess what window it had been.

Right then, a yellow cab pulled up outside the building's entrance and a uniformed doorman rushed out ahead of an elegantly-clad middle-aged woman wearing an expensive-looking fur coat and held the cab's door open for her. Leonard felt something was familiar about the woman. A faint degree of recognition in the way she stood ramrod straight with the fluid composure of a ballet dancer.

There was another cab, going in the opposite direction, cruising down the street with it light on. He hailed it and it made a rapid U-turn.

'Can you follow that taxi over there?' he asked the driver. He was half expecting him to respond with a bad joke, or something about him having watched too many movies, but the guy just nodded, too busy listening to a cacophony of loud reggae music on his headphones.

The midday traffic was heavy as the two cabs, just a few vehicles apart, inched their way towards 5th and then proceeded towards downtown.

Eventually, the cab he was following turned right when it reached Washington Square and finally came to a halt outside an Italian restaurant on Waverly Place. The woman exited and entered the restaurant. Leonard asked his own driver to stop, which he did outside a hotel on the other side of the street, paid and stood for a moment, pondering his next step. To wait for the woman outside in the cold, just walk a few blocks further south to his rental apartment as he was now fortuitously almost back home or just give up altogether.

A group of Dutch tourists leaving the hotel he was

standing next to jostled him as they rolled their luggage down the stone steps he was unknowingly blocking. Leonard moved aside, apologising and, on a whim, crossed the road and walked into the restaurant.

'Do you have a reservation, Sir?'

The warm atmosphere of the restaurant surrounded him, alongside the smell of food and spices.

'I'm afraid not. I just came in on the off chance.'

The greeter looked down at her reservation book, and then looked up at him with an insincere smile.

'You're in luck, Sir. I do have a table for two left.'

'It's just me. I am not expecting a guest.'

'That's no problem.'

She led him through the busy dining room to a small table by the backwall.

Sitting down, he looked around. The woman from the Marseilles Building was at another table for two just across from him, busy effusively chatting with another woman, older, also expensively dressed, her grey hair carefully sculpted into an imposing chignon. There was a distinct similarity in their features, as if the older woman was a future portrait of her interlocutor. Her mother?

He was handed a menu but declined the wine list and ordered a mineral water, while trying to make up his mind, searching through the list for something not likely to be smothered in tomato sauce. He finally opted for a salad of artichoke hearts and spinach followed by the vitello tonato, having scouted the menu in vain for the seafood he normally fancied.

The conversations buzzed all around him and he was unable to eavesdrop much into the two women's dialogue, as they both spoke quietly or more often spent the time in meaningful silences, the sort of half conversations only folk who had known each for a long time sustained. Married couples, family.

Formulating a vague plan, he made his meal last, waiting to see whether the two women would leave the restaurant together or part at the door. He was by habit of having lived alone now for several years a rapid eater so it didn't prove easy and he had to stretch the meal with two espresso coffees in a row, as the women lingered over their food and the dining room crowd thinned down.

Finally, their table cleared and both having made leisurely pilgrimages to the powder room, the older woman flashed her credit card. Leonard called for his own check.

He exited the restaurant just ahead of the two women, his hanging around, he hoped, unnoticed on the other side of the road, again by the entrance of the boutique hotel that stood there, standing anonymous amongst the tourists coming and going.

The two women, now swathed in their heavy winter garments, embraced and separated, going in opposite directions. The mother towards 6th Avenue and the subway on the street's corner, the younger woman, right now his prey, steadily making her way along the park. He had expected her to hail a passing cab, but she ignored them all and crossed University Place, heading towards Broadway. He followed her at a short distance, his senses in overdrive, stimulated by all the accumulated caffeine he had consumed while keeping a watch on her. Not a good idea.

She took Broadway North and walked into the Strand Bookstore. Here, she initially navigated the new hardcover titles table, picking up a volume here and there and quickly rejecting them all once she had read the inside flap or back cover blurbs.

She didn't appear to be searching for a particular title, though. Showing some signs of impatience, she then retreated, walking back onto Broadway. She buttoned up her full-length fur coat as the cold air wrapped itself around her and he assumed she would call a cab, but she just stepped a few meters up and entered the adjacent building. He knew the Strand's Rare Book Room was situated on the 3rd floor of the building. He'd visited it on many occasions during the time he was working in book publishing. It must be her destination.

There was an exiguous elevator but he deemed it preferable not to share it with her. Nor to walk up the steep stairs he remembered. He watched from the pavement as she waited for the elevator to arrive. Then stepped in to the building and waited for the elevator to return. He would only miss her if she had a change of mind and once she had reached the 3rd floor, suddenly decided to use the stairs on her way down. Which he deemed unlikely. The Rare Book Room was a place you spent time in, unless you were only there to pick something up you'd ordered previously.

He walked into the wide high-ceilinged room and was assaulted by the familiar smell of books, paper and dust. Floor to ceiling shelves covered every inch of wall, and glass cabinets and tables were scattered across the polished, wooden floor.

The woman in the fur coat was browsing at the table displaying signed copies and advance proofs.

Was she a collector? Leonard realised this was a unique opportunity to maybe interact. In a place like this, talking about books would not necessarily be considered intrusive.

He approached the table and, across from her, casually picked up a signed Lee Child advance proof. She failed to note his presence, absorbed by a modern first she was leafing through. He squinted, trying to read its title, as he couldn't recognise the dust jacket. It then came into focus and he realised why the book was unfamiliar: it was a US edition and he was more familiar with the British incarnation. 'The White Hotel' by D.M. Thomas.

'A wonderful novel,' he said.

She looked up at him, her thoughts interrupted.

'It is indeed. I have in fact read it a long while ago, but at the time I could only afford paperbacks ... So I was just curious to have a look at this version. Rather expensive, don't you think?'

He took note of the price the Strand were asking for the Mylar polyester-protected volume.

It was. He was surprised it wasn't locked away in one of

the cabinets.

'At this stage in a novel or a movie, I'd offer to purchase it for you and shrug and say it was nothing when your face turned pink with embarrassment ...'

'No need to,' she smiled. 'We're civilised adults. No need for fiction or pretence. But it certainly would have been an elegant opening gambit for a game of seduction, no?'

'It would have been, but I'm not sure I can afford the gesture. I've also become, for my sins, a paperback sort of guy.'

She set the volume down on the table next to the other expensive offerings on display.

Looking him straight in the eye, she said 'You were also at the restaurant, weren't you?'

'Guilty.' He was in no position to deny it.

'And you followed me here?'

'Guilty again ...'

'Don't say it's because you admire my taste in books.'

He could feel her mischievously playing with him.

'Had I known I would have done so there, but I fear approaching you during your meal with your friend to, say, comment about the food would have been a severe breach of etiquette.'

'My mother, not my friend. We are not in fact on great terms right now; I won't bore you with the details. And she would have disapproved of such a rude public intervention. She is old-fashioned that way.'

'Hence my following you here ...'

'At least you are a man with some knowledge of books. Not many of those left around. An analogue man in a digital world.'

'I once worked in publishing.'

'How convenient. So why did you follow me?'

Was she aware he had already been on her trail well before she had arrived at the Waverly Place restaurant?

'A spur of the moment thing ...'

'Ah, an impulsive man!'

'Just something about you,' he lied.

'Ah, flattery. Man's ultimate weapon of choice …'

'So, might you require further book recommendations? I'd be happy to help,' he asked.

'Probably not,' she ruled. 'Maybe we should just skip the preliminaries?'

'I'd love that. I'm Leonard, by the way.'

'Violet,' She extended her hand. He shook it. 'But, regrettably, my maker didn't go so far as to grant me the same colour eyes as my name.'

They were actually green. A most striking shade against the pallor of her skin. Leonard couldn't remember whether violet and green were in fact complementary colours in the order of things.

'Glad to have met you.'

'Oh, come on, don't be so modest. You engineered the encounter, didn't you? I don't believe in coincidence.'

He maintained a polite silence, unsure whether she was toying with him or he was misinterpreting her barbed irony. How long could he sustain this game and not drop his guard?

The window through which he had first caught a glimpse of her was her bedroom's. Which made sense because of the time of night when he had made his way to Carlotta Valdes's apartment in the building opposite.

But now it was only mid-afternoon and, outside, snow had begun to fall on the Manhattan pavements. Fall had passed into winter. Heavy flakes, damp, like the sky's afterthought. It wouldn't settle and later the streets would be rife with sludge. It occurred to him he was wearing the wrong kind of shoes and his loafers would get ruined. Oh well …

He was standing by the bed, half daydreaming, half wondering how it had come to his. Violet had excused herself and gone to the bathroom down the hall. On arriving at the apartment, she had led him straight to the bedroom, given him a peck on the cheek, dropped her heavy fur coat to the carpeted floor, and kicked off her high heel pumps, revealing a sharp red-coloured sole. Louboutin or imitation? Then stepped away. To adjust her make-up, change, tidy herself up? She was wearing a white, opaque silk shirt and high-waisted tailored navy trousers. The shirt was loose, the trousers tight around the contours of her arse. He liked the way she filled her clothes. She had raised a finger to her lips, as if ordering him to keep quiet, as now was no longer the time for dialogue or banter. Just action?

His attention was drawn past the window to the facing building and he tried to locate the small balcony. It could have been one of three on the façade. Not that it mattered. What did was how much she could have seen that night, if indeed she was accidentally watching at the right time. Or would it be better described as the wrong time? As afternoon progresses, the quality of light outside changes.

He felt her breath on his neck. She had returned silently to the bedroom, now standing by his side, green forest-like notes in her scent. He turned his head towards her. Tried to say something but she quickly shushed him and their lips met.

The heat of her body, like a fire ready to consume him.

The taste of her tongue.

The drawn-out sound of her breathing.

His hand on her waist.

Her trousered knee parting his legs, forcing him open as if she was the aggressor.

The uncontrolled beat of his heart, remembering what it felt to be with a woman for the first time. With fear, tremulous joy, terrible expectations and the electric streams of desire bursting past the dam of what was left of his respectability. Feelings he once had been a slave to, hopelessly addicted to, dependent on, an ambivalent and not always welcome aspect of what made him who he was.

Giving in to her kiss, he had thrown a final glance at the window and she somehow intuited what he was looking at. Their lips parted.

'Such a great view, no? One of the reasons I moved into

this apartment.' She sounded amused, probing for a reaction.

He ignored her, his right hand gently pulling the bottom of her white linen shirt from the trousers' waistband.

But why did he feel that she was the one seducing him, the party in charge?

Falling to the bed. Clothes being pulled off. The landscape of her taut body, her painted nails grazing the sensitive skin of his cock as she pulled him out of his boxers, her breath syncopating in unison with his as the lust rose.

Limbs forced aside, opened.

Her lips pressed against his, smothering him, a hand pulling on his hair to bring him even closer. Her hard nipples digging into his chest, her free hand below tugging at him, hastening his hardness. She was now the predator and he the prey. He wanted to protest, but she had made it clear she was now running the show and would take her pleasure by hook or by crook. Any moment now, he expected her to become verbal, ordering him around like some petty sexual subaltern. They had barely spoken since the moment she had invited him to her apartment, as if she knew words were unnecessary, that they had moved far beyond that stage in their particular dance of lust.

She was going to take what she wanted, and he would have no say in the matter. Her pleasure was paramount. He was just a man with the right equipment, a body, a cock.

A small voice inside his head suggested he should interrupt this one-way flow. Maybe assert himself more, refuse to be used, pull her down to the bed and spread her thighs apart and go down on her as a way of reasserting control.

But she beat him to it.

She unbuttoned his shirt, her fingers tiptoeing almost negligently across his own nipples. Hot touch. A flash of electricity moving from finger to chest.

She briefly fell to her knees and took him into her mouth, as if to verify his hardness rather than afford him pleasure and then satisfied by the texture and girth of his erection, she dropped to the bed still pulling on his cock and settled herself on all fours, facing away from him, presenting him with her fleshy rump.

'Mount me,' she ordered him.

He did.

They had sex. Furious and fast and dirty as he impaled her with a heart full of rage.

It wasn't making love, but an animalistic ritual that must have originated in the depths of time when man and woman mated in the mud, the grass, under canopies of trees.

They fucked.

He groaned.

She moaned.

It was fast. Selfish. Each racing for release with no consideration for the other.

He had loved, slept with many women, but this was different. Filthy, pornographic, rough, liberating.

Later, both out of breath, sweat still abundant and pearling down their backs, their feet tangling with the soiled sheets, the sky outside the window now dark as, night and the moon nowhere to be seen over the Park, they fell silent. Both observing the room's landscape after the battle, feeling like strangers.

'You were pretty good,' Violet said. A verdict delivered.

'The least I could do to honour you, Madam.'

'How polite you English are ...'

'We aim to please.'

She was spreadeagled across her side of the bed, his attention drawn to the fact her pubic delta was a shade darker than her hair, although he had been hypnotised earlier whilst implacably ploughing her as she called for him to dig deeper and harder and have no mercy with her, by the thin layer of blonde down in the delta formed by the junction between her long, elongated back and her arse.

'Anyway, I owed you that, I suppose ...'

'What do you mean?' he queried.

'Call it a tip ... or do you Brits call it a gratuity?'

'I'm not sure I understand.'

'Don't you?'

'I'm baffled.'

Violet laughed.

'What's so funny?'

'I know exactly who you are.'

Leonard felt a shiver run down a spine.

'You saw me on the balcony? You recognised me?'

'Of course, I did. I watched you at work. And very efficient you were. I knew who you were the moment you walked into Babbo's. At first I thought it was one of those quirky coincidences, but I saw you kept on looking over to our table, and then it made sense. You were concerned I had witnessed you killing that bitch Valdes.'

'And you had …'

'No worry, I have no intention of calling the police.'

'That sounds rather perverse. Why?'

'Because I ordered the kill.'

'What the hell?'

She stretched her limbs.

'I think I need a shower now.'

'You knew all along and took me for a ride?'

'Oh, come on. Didn't you enjoy having me?'

He reluctantly nodded. Although he now realised she was the one who had been using him.

'Now if you don't mind, I'll have to wash you off me for good. New experience, I must say, fucking a killer. But you're just a man. Although nicely educated and articulate; that did come as a pleasant surprise …'

Again, he felt, she was toying with him.

'Why did you want her dead?'

'Ah, it's just business. No concern of yours.'

'Is it about the Continental? Trafficking the dancers?'

'What's the Continental? No, as I said, just business matters you don't have to know anything about.'

'I see,' he felt let down, cheated.

'But now if you'll excuse me, I have to wash and tidy up

before my husband gets home. He should be here by eight. So I'd rather you picked up your clothes and left.'

Leonard sighed and slipped off the bed, retrieving his abandoned clothing from the floor.

'And of course, we will never meet again.'

The bathroom door slammed shut behind her.

Never had he felt so used. Or confused.

8
Murder on the Dance Floor

He roamed Manhattan like the ghost of himself. He'd looked at his face in the bathroom mirror that morning and was shocked to note a hollowness in both his cheeks he had not previously been aware of. He knew it couldn't have happened overnight and that he was eating properly, so just a normal process of ageing he guessed. But worrying. He had never been much of a cheerful person, and his smiles were carefully rationed, but he felt he now looked gaunt, his features under assault from the natural ravages of time. It wasn't just the small pains in his body: his left knee, the increasing weakness in his right eye, the spasm that sometimes dug like a dagger on the side of his thigh. He was not a happy man.

He was going round in circles, revisiting places he knew inside out, avoiding others, like a loose atom set loose on the inner city, bouncing from one pole to another with no sense of destination or logic. Although it made no sense, he felt like a veteran rock'n'roller embarking on his farewell tour, one that lasts forever.

Georgia and her baby hadn't been seen at Wanda's Café for over two weeks. Trisha had no idea where they might be, but assured Leonard there was no reason to worry. It was something Georgia did, appearing, reappearing in cycles with a rationale of their own.

'She's young,' she said, as if it was an excuse.

'But what about the child?' he queried. 'Where does she get the money to feed it? She has no job.'

Trisha frowned.

'Maybe best not to enquire …'

'What does that mean?'

'It means what it means.'

His mind travelled back to the taxi dancers and the possibility some or all were being trafficked. He just couldn't imagine young Georgia peddling her body. The possibility alone was just too awful. Or her relying on some sordid sugar daddy in the downtown wilderness. Kris, the disbarred cop, had taken it upon himself to be her protector. Where was he now? One of the regulars said he had returned to Oregon, seeking some sort of solace in the mountains. Had he come to the conclusion he couldn't save Georgia and succumbed to despair and flight? Leonard couldn't help himself imagine stories for all those people he barely knew. He couldn't avoid it. It was the way his imagination worked. But why did so many of these stories he spun dip into the dirtier side of society and did he attribute tales of fallen debauchery and degradation to his barely imagined characters?

Was his mind contaminated? Sullied beyond redemption?

Like a black hole at the very centre of his peregrinations, The Continental Ballroom was the one place he now carefully avoided. A small voice inside advising him to keep clear.

He picked up a two days old New York Post someone had discarded, from a nearby table at the café. Browsed through it, his mind on other things until he reached the New Jersey local news page and his heart stopped beating and his throat ran dry. A photograph.

Meg.

He recognised her immediately, even though it was probably a few years old and was a poor ID pic paused against a neutral white background, her eyes glazed by the camera's flash, unsmiling. The photo had evidently been taken for her passport or driving license application.

He felt paralysed. Unwilling, fearful to move his eyes just that inch south to read the accompanying headline.

He forced himself to look down.

MISSING HEIRESS BODY PARTS IDENTIFIED

He felt sick.

Stood up unsteadily, stumbled to the washroom, and threw

up, bile rising up his throat in a bitter torrent.

Remained there for what felt like an eternity, reluctant to return to the café and read the rest of the article.

Tried to get his nerves under control. Had to move his hand to the wall to counter his dizziness.

'Are you OK, my love?'

'Yes, I just felt a bit faint there for a moment …'

'I'll bring you some water.'

'There is no need. I still have my soda.'

He was half-hoping someone might have disposed of the newspaper in his absence, but it still lay there open on the table, the unflattering photo of Meg leading the feature.

He took a hold of himself, composed his expression into a semblance of normality and began reading, every line a stiletto piercing his gut.

Despite her initial claim to the contrary, she was actually called Megan. Megan Irish. She was the daughter of a wealthy Canadian aerospace industrialist now based in Oakland in California. She had been missing for over a month, had lived in Brooklyn on her own but was reported to be often away from her home on business, although neither neighbour or family had any idea what she was involved in. Her relatives in Oakland, had raised the alarm after she had failed to return there for a significant family celebration. Her passport had been found in a drawer of her bedside table and showed recent travel to Germany and Spain.

A week earlier a suitcase had been fished out of the Hudson and the cut up remains of a woman were found inside, although her head was missing.

A postmortem examination had determined she had died by a severe ligature to her throat and the body had been quartered several days following her death. Although her teeth had been extracted to avoid dental records identification and her fingertips burned, two fingers had been accidentally spared and a set of fingerprints lifted, though the authorities had held little hope of finding out who the body parts had belonged to. However, Megan had fingerprints on record, from her teenage years' minor narcotics arrest.

The family was understandably distraught and investigations were ongoing, although the reporter who had signed the feature speculated about organised crime involvement, although the cruelty and savagery of Megan Irish's circumstances had been considered a thing of the past. But the white upper-class background of the glamorous victim was certainly puzzling and untypical. The hack further catalogued similar crimes from the archive, including the infamous Black Dahlia case, based on tenuous information gleaned from acquaintances of Megan Irish that she had once loved flowers.

Leonard gulped again, the bile now flooding his mouth and headed for the washroom.

He was sick in the basin, expelling all his bitterness and then began sobbing. His body in the grip of nausea and his guilt unleashed.

He waited impatiently for days for the people from the Bureau to contact him again. Rehearsing in his mind the many questions he wanted to ask them about Meg, his anger, fury and recriminations at what they appeared to have done to her, with her. It was unconscionable, downright barbaric and he wanted to make them pay. But how?

In the Bureau's eyes, what she had done by involving him in her assignment had been a bad mistake, but surely then killing her outright with a view to forcing him to become a replacement was a step too far.

He raged as he remembered the obscene vision of her dead body spreadeagled across his hotel bed and could barely contain his rage at the thought of how she had been desecrated later.

But then, he realised, the Bureau knew all too well how disposing of a body, particularly so in a teeming metropolis that never slept like New York, was a challenge. Gone were the mafia days of encasing human remains in the concrete of new buildings, or had that only happened in the movies? Or dissolving them in acid in bathtubs. Too messy. And how did you get the body out of the hotel? A suitcase of course.

How could he prove so understanding? Because they had turned him to a killer himself, and his mind was now thinking that way. He hated the Bureau and he hated himself.

But the phone wouldn't ring.

And the only messages on the apartment's recording service were for his travelling, overseas landlord.

He attentively followed the case in the Post, but no further facts emerged and within a week it appeared to be already forgotten. Old news. Even though the suitcase had been destined for a suitable ending at the bottom of the Hudson River, it washing up on the Jersey shore made little difference. The Bureau and its sinister minions left no clues to hazard. Maybe one day, the story would see the light of day again in a true crime blog. 'The Heiress in the Suitcase'. Leonard hated true crime blogs. Considered most of them exploitative, immoral. Jumpers on a voyeuristic bandwagon. But who was he now to talk of morality, no paragon of virtue by a long stretch?

But still he would hurry down most mornings to the corner Bodega on Spring and Sullivan to pick up the newspaper, which he would carefully leaf through in search of possible news. Which is where he came across a quarter page advertisement for the Continental's forthcoming dance marathon, with the lure of a vacation in Palm Springs for the lucky couple who would emerge the winners at the end of a gruelling 24 hours of non-stop dancing. Nothing like reviving old traditions, he reckoned. Would the participants be asked to dress in depression chic? Leonard wondered whether any of the taxi dancers would be involved, coupled up with needy boyfriends, or sugar daddies with ulterior motives and enough stamina to survive the dance floor Armageddon. He felt a strange fascination for the place and its unworldly events, a sick attraction which didn't help him feel any better about entertaining such lurid thoughts.

He had become a man severed from joy, he knew. And without the slightest prospect of ever finding it again, that elusive feeling that would soothe his soul, and not just his loins. Stolen from him forever.

He hadn't shaved for several days. Just couldn't be bothered. Nor had he washed his hair for a week. Aways wore the same shapeless cargo pants and a grey sweatshirt; sometimes even slept in them. Hiding from the world; a world in which he somehow no longer fitted.

The phone rang.

A rush of anxiety spiralled through his body.

Another job?

He picked the receiver up.

Within a few seconds he realised it was just a call centre, trying to sell him insurance or healthcare. He slammed the phone down long before they could complete their pitch.

Looked around his rental apartment. Felt hemmed in, a prisoner of its walls, grabbed his overcoat, and walked down the narrow, badly lit stairs instead of using the elevator and found himself on the street. Hesitated. North to the West Village or South towards Little Italy or Chinatown?

It was too early to catch a movie and something was keeping him away from Wanda's Café.

He wandered up Broadway and then realised it was Sunday and many of the stores weren't even open, not that he had planned searching for or buying anything. It was a cloudless day with patches of occasional blue peering out from behind the moving banks of clouds, and the air was crisp and cold, bracing even as he heartily filled his lungs, now walking faster, his pitiful excuse for exercise until half a dozen blocks later, he had to slow down, running out of breath and the damn pain in his left knee awakening. He was now close to the New York Public Library and Bryant Park and once there found a seat by a deserted carousel, and gazed at the manicured lawn circled by the empty walkways. It felt like a momentary haven of peace, a haven from the often-relentless noise of the surrounding city.

With a sigh of nostalgia, he recalled attending a wedding reception and dinner at the nearby library for some distant relatives of his wife. The meal had been a shameless display of opulence paid for by the bride's wealthy plastic surgeon parents from Florida, no doubt grateful she had found herself a professor of politics just in time before reaching the age of 30. There had been over 20 tables laid out across the room, each decorated by monstrously large imitation Fabergé eggs which had been sculpted out of chocolate and then decorated, Along the back walls, additional tables had been laid out with cascades of fruit and enormous cheese plates that any Frenchman would have envied, although by the time the meal had reached that stage, following the main courses, the mother of the groom's singing at the piano and much too many speeches, half of which by an assortment of rabbis, neither Leonard nor his wife had any appetite to even touch the cheese.

How many years ago had that been? Long before her illness had manifested itself fully. There had been moments of forgetfulness, inattention, and sudden mood swings, but it had all been part and parcel of everyday married life and he hadn't given it further consideration. Until the day when, returning from New Year's Eve in New Orleans, the weather had disrupted journeys and their delayed flight had been diverted to Houston where they had to wait half a day for a connection to New York. Their concourse was bursting at the seams with travellers and they finally managed to find two seats together at one end, and sat there waiting for a favourable announcement, reading, daydreaming. She had to go to the washroom; normally because of her occasional lapses, he would accompany her to the door of the ladies, in restaurants, stores, and wait for her outside. Today, his tiredness and the fact that the toilets were just a stone's throw away from where they had settled down, he opted to leave her to her own devices as he could watch the exit of the relevant washroom from his seat and wave her over, should she appear disorientated. However, he had missed her actual exit from the facility, distracted by the book he was reading and she had somehow wandered off in the wrong direction. By the time he realised what might have happened, she was already wandering through the airport seeking him out, without her passport, her ticket or anything that might help her locate the gate he was sitting at. Eventually, he had to find an airport employee and arrange for an announcement on the Tannoy. She was missing for nearly two hours, no doubt in an abject state of panic, as was he; fortunately their new flight wasn't called, or they would have been left stranded in Houston without their luggage. Eventually, she was found and he had to walk over to a desk on a separate concourse, where two members of staff were looking after her in fear she might go wandering off again. It's then Leonard realised he had a major problem.

He now sat in Bryant Park, feeling colder by the minute, his mind a prisoner of the past.

No, he had never been angry at her when she had her episodes, although as the dementia worsened she was often the one who would become aggressive, evoking their past and accusing him of so many things he had never done. Never the things he had. Turning jealous at the drop of a feather, accusing him of having affairs with women, acquaintances he barely knew, belittling the work he did.

It lasted several years. He had looked after her, cooked for her, chosen daily what she would wear, dressed her, mopped up the floor in the corridor or the spare bedroom next to theirs, when she had woken in the middle of the night and forgotten where the toilet was and peed, or worse, where she stood, uncertain of her surroundings in the house she had lived in now for decades.

Later, she would lose the power of speech and begin babbling like a baby as her brain began to disenfranchise itself from her body and her functions. She stayed in bed all day and had to be fed, slowly, carefully, like a baby. No solids in case she choked on something.

He had stood by. Helpless.

So why was he now the one feeling guilt. And on the run. From what?

'Is that you?'

He looked up.

A young woman's face. Which he didn't immediately recognise. Although, on second thought, there was something a little familiar about her but he couldn't pinpoint the connection. Rosy cheeks and freckles dotting her forehead and perky nose. A pronounced Southern accent. Maybe New Orleans area?

She noted his perplexity.

'I know the lighting at the ballroom does no one any favours! I'm Ruby Rose ... Used to work at the bar there. We spoke once.'

'Ah!' he acknowledged her presence.

She wore jogging shorts, a tight black T-shirt advertising some rock band he'd vaguely heard about and thick-soled trendy running shoes. In the flesh, she was diminutive, almost half the size she had appeared to be behind the Continental Bar.

'I remember you now, yes, at the bar ...'

'You were asking lots of questions. About the dancers, the manager ... But you didn't ... don't look like a cop.'

'Yes, that was me. So how come our paths cross again? Or is it an accident?'

'I was out jogging,' she pointed at her apparel. 'Duh. I always take a halfway stage break in Bryant Park, before I saunter back to Alphabet City. That's where I live, in New York that is.'

'Quite a coincidence meeting here. In fact, it's the very first time I've set foot in the park. But I'm not a jogger, I fear.'

'That's somehow evident,' Ruby Rose shrugged, looking across at what he was wearing.

'Do you want to sit down?' There was space for another on the narrow wooden bench.

She hesitated. 'I suppose I'm not on the clock. Why not?'

She had been sweating heavily. He liked the musky scent of her immediate presence.

'So did I hear right: you no longer work at the Continental?'

'Yeah, gave up on that dump weeks ago. It was going nowhere. And there were bad vibes. I never saw myself making a career of serving in a bar, anyway ...'

'So, what do you do now?'

'This and that,' Ruby Rose said. 'Thinking I might go back to school next fall. Back home.'

'Where's home?'

'Baton Rouge in Louisiana.'

His earlier guess had not relatively been geographically distant.

'And you?'

'Me what?'

'What do you do? For work. Or are you a gentleman of leisure?'

He had to quickly think on his feet.

'I'm a book dealer. Sort of freelance. It's complicated.'

'Do people still read books?'

'They do, surprisingly enough.'

'Ah ...'

'You don't?'

'Only when I had to for school. Life is there to be lived, you know?'

'It's a matter of opinion ...' He had no wish to enter into a petty dispute right now, let alone with Ruby Rose.

Silence settled.

Both hesitant to break it.

He was the one to speak first.

'Want to have a coffee, or something stronger?'

'Actually, why not? I ain't much of a coffee drinker. However early in the day I have one it will keep me awake at night ... And I don't drink, so if you know of a place nearby when we can have tea, that would be great.'

135

'A barmaid who doesn't drink!'

'Pretty much an involuntary barmaid,' she pointed out. 'They only gave me the job out of pity, as I wasn't good enough for the dancing.'

'Yes, I recall.'

They rose from the bench in unison.

It was approaching the lunch hour and the Midtown diners were filling up, mostly with tourists from the multitude of huge hotels in the neighbourhood. He had a suggestion: 'There is a nice bar at the Grand Central Terminal.' There would be few businessmen frequenting the place on a Sunday.

'Wow. Is that where the famous Oyster Bar is?'

'The one and the same.'

'Is it expensive?'

'My treat, Miss Ruby Rose who doesn't read books.'

He knew the only reason he was sticking it out with her was that he was lonely and had no desire to keep on treading the pavements on his own, lost in unpalatable thoughts about his past mistakes, lost women and self-hate.

And maybe she would let something slip about the mysteries of the Continental Ballroom from her time spent working there?

Was Patrice, the manager, still working there or had there been significant changes following the inopportune death of Carlotta Valdes?

She jokingly suggested they might jog all the way there together but he declined. No way would he have been capable of keeping up with her, he pretexted. In fact, he never ran anywhere these days.

'You old man, you,' she laughed.

Once at the station, they descended the majestic stairs only to find out the Oyster Bar didn't open at the weekend.

'Ah, men,' sighed Ruby Rose. 'You always let us down.'

He apologized profusely and they then walked over to the Algonquin Hotel on 44th where the bar seemed to never close. Leonard felt an unwelcome twinge in his lower stomach, glancing over at the door of the other hotel right across 44th

Street, in which he had once stayed and Meg's body was left in his room. The doorman looked down at the way Ruby Rose was dressed but let them in with a shrug. It wasn't his fault that New York was now awash with joggers and the venerable hotel has long since dispensed with a rigorous dress code, forced to move along with the times.

The bar was famous but in Leonard's opinion too well lit. Surely, bars must harbour a measure of darkness to create an atmosphere of not just conviviality but also the potential for more, a prelude to seduction or drunkenness? He didn't enjoy being in the spotlight. He didn't fit in this sort of environment any longer. And neither did Ruby Rose, regardless of her jogging gear. She wasn't a creature bred for high society. Maybe not the gutter, but the shadier side of life. Or was he underestimating her? He hardly knew the young girl and was still suspicious of running into her in Bryant Park. Was it too much of a coincidence?

He wanted to talk about her days at the Continental. Seeking out answers, clues.

'So you no longer work there?' he asked her.

'Yeah, not a healthy scene, you know.' A faint smile spread across her lips, below her button nose. 'Was offered a job, a bit of admin and all that, at a hipster bar on Lafayette, just off Astor Place.'

'How come unhealthy?'

'Didn't you notice?'

'Not really, I was too busy dancing, watching the dancers ...' he excused himself, although he realised it might make him sound like just a dirty old perv.

'Drugs, stuff ... All over the place ... Easily available. Discreet but frequent.'

'Oh,' he truly hadn't realised.

'And I'm a bit too partial to the softer stuff myself, so too many temptations. There were days, evenings when my resolve was sorely tested ... I'm aware of my weaknesses and the slippery slope ahead.' That complicit smile again.

How could he have been so blind to the obvious? He'd only had eyes for Helen and not peered beyond.

'What about you?' she glanced inquisitively at him.

'Me what?'

'The recreational stuff ... Do you indulge?'

'Not my scene, or taste,' he responded. 'I'm more of a sex, books and rock'n'roll sort of guy ...' He smiled.

She appeared impassive. Maybe the wrong generation to appreciate his joke, he guessed.

As a matter of fact, he had never been much attracted to that side of things. Naturally, when younger, he had been curious, although where he lived at the time and in the circles he frequented, the opportunities to sample soft drugs had been limited; it was more of a booze milieu. Eventually, he'd tried pot, but like smoking tobacco, its only effect had been mildly unpleasant and in no way to his taste. Later, with an illustrator friend, they had one empty week-end managed to get hold of some acid. A small square of blotting paper allegedly soaked in LSD which Michel had obtained from a friend of a friend at the Paris radio station where he worked. They had studiously cut the portion into two halves of the same size and gulped theirs down. And then waited. Half an hour later, the acid still hadn't taken effect and they had assumed Michel had been sold a dud. Sighing in disappointment, and with an empty evening facing them, they agreed to play a game of poker, one of their occasional Saturday night killing time activity. Neither could afford to play for cash, so they used matchsticks. It was too late to catch a movie in the Latin Quarter. Another hour passed, and Leonard noticed that Michel not only was losing fairly steadily, but unlike his usual self was not loudly protesting about it. A marked sign that he wasn't truly himself. Accepting his losses with uncommon serenity. Was it the effect of the LSD? Leonard, however, felt nothing. Then Michel threw his cards down and moaned that he was feeling unsteady and unable to concentrate.

It became a memorable night. While the dose of acid they had ingested took hold of Michel with ferocity, Leonard remained disappointingly untouched by its spread across his consciousness, as his friend plunged headlong into a ferocious trip, in which the walls of the room, he groaned, were undulating, closing him in, suffocating him.

Leonard became his friend's babysitter and protector from the ongoing waves of nightmares he unwittingly travelled through, sitting there by his side, holding him, his hands, reassuring him, towelling his sweat, while all along he remained supremely unaffected.

The following morning, after his shaken buddy had left for his own apartment, Leonard found himself sitting there, feeling empty, in the knowledge that he was somehow immune to pot and acid, unable to enjoy some of the same pleasures of life available to others. It was sobering. Maybe his own chemical make-up, the nature of his physiology was askew, inhibiting the action of particular stimulants?

It could have been a short story: 'The man whose chemical make-up veered one degree too far to the left' …

Some years later, he was presented at the Frankfurt Book Fair with the opportunity to sample cocaine, but he had by then lost all his curiosity about soft drugs and politely declined.

Possibly by now he had come to the conclusion that women and sex were, as far as he was concerned, a more interesting stimulant than alcohol, tobacco and drugs! Though this often meant that he was not always at his most entertaining in social circumstances, preferring the intimacy of one-to-one conversations to the superficiality of crowds.

'At the Continental, all over bloody Manhattan, the fucking stuff is everywhere,' Ruby Rose protested, as she sipped her hot chocolate. 'Not a good place for me. I've lost friends and acquaintances; that's why I think I'll soon be heading home.'

'Were some of the dime dancers dealing?' he asked her.

'Absolutely. Most of them were.'

'Of their own accord or was the management of the

ballroom involved?'

'Of course. They supplied the stuff. If a girl went freelance, found herself an outside supplier, she was promptly booted out, or worse.'

'Were many of them?' he asked.

'What?'

'Was it frequent for dancers to be caught selling drugs not controlled by the Continental, and shown the door or punished?'

'It happened.'

'Do you remember any names?'

He was still hoping to pinpoint what might have happened to Helen.

'No. I no longer had much contact with the dancing girls once I moved behind the bar. I hadn't made the grade in their ranks and most looked down on me. I was never friends with any of them, really.'

Their conversation ground to a slow halt; as they both came to the realisation neither had much more to say to the other. Or ask. Visibly, Leonard concluded, their crossing paths in Bryant Park was just a coincidence.

They parted. Wishing each other well. It was only two in the afternoon; the weekend still had a long way to go. They didn't exchange telephone numbers.

Never had Leonard felt so alone and despairing of his future. In fact, as he reflected, sitting on his sofa watching the patterns of the outside light mutate from shape to shape on the opposing wall, it wasn't a future at all. Just an emptiness.

He tried to read a book, but his mind just couldn't settle and the characters and the action unfolding on the pages were too tenuous to grasp or, at any rate, evince any interest.

He listened to music but again he was unfocused, finding little recognition or pleasure in melodies, songs, singers, bands that once he had unconsciously tapped his feet to or sung along to, his heart opening up to their subtle magic.

Months ago, it had felt like that at home in London. It was the reason he had begun travelling again. Searching. For something. For a reason to keep hanging on.

And, briefly, it had.

The sights, sounds and smells of new places. The setting of the sun across the distant horizon of a faraway beach, the initial coldness of the sea as he tiptoed into it barefoot, the taste of fresh seafood laid out like a feast for the senses across a colourful table. The pungency and balance of spices in a crawfish boil, the gooey potency of a well-made busy gumbo, the marine taste of freshly shucked oysters, the animalistic, raw vigour of a steak tartare or the simple pleasure of slices of sashimi sprinkled in soya sauce. Gifts to the senses.

But even those simple pleasures proved ephemeral.

And then the anomie returned. Heavy. Grounded. A sense of inevitability and uselessness.

His mind swirled, every single thought fighting against each other, leaving him exhausted and empty every single time.

Was this all he could look forward to?

It was Sunday. Wanda's Café would be closed.

There was nothing on Netflix or any of the streaming platforms that excited his curiosity.

He kept on returning to the same conclusion: he was a boring man with no future, overloaded with guilt and sorrow. In books, it would have sounded romantic; in reality, it was nothing of the kind. Just sad and pitiful.

At least he could look forward to the phone ringing with a call from the Bureau.

A target.

A job.

Soon, he hoped.

Someone to kill. And keep him busy and his mind distracted from the abyss he was wallowing in. And refresh his coffers, as the money from previous jobs was now running low, rent and such in Manhattan not being on the cheap side

Murder would give him a new purpose in life.

It wasn't perfect, but it was all he had.

9

The Sadness of the Short Distance Hitman

It was early March. The days went on forever, the nights ever endless.

An assignment finally came.

Leonard had been hoping for a job that might involve substantial travel; more than he had done on any previous job. He wanted new horizons, a break from Manhattan and its ghosts and coincidences.

But again, it was local.

He studied the dossier and requested Hopley's assistance. He would have welcomed some additional advice to work out the likely logistics of the hit. But he was informed that Hopley was no longer attached to the Bureau and no further contact was advised. This didn't come as a total surprise. He quietly hoped it had been the man's personal decision, but he harboured doubts. After what had happened to Meg, he knew being a facilitator for the Bureau also entailed proving disposable.

That same evening, he lost a front tooth biting into a square of dark chocolate, leaving him with an unattractive gap. He had never been much of a smiler and knew that over the years he had signally neglected his teeth and was now reaping the due reward but took the event with resignation, and a further acceptance of his mortality or rather his physical decay now meekly imitating the frayed condition of his tired mind. He made no immediate plans to see a dentist.

Fortunately, there was no time limit attached to the job on this occasion, and he took advantage of this, studying the pages and photographs he had been provided with in forensic detail, mulling over locations, methods and likely pitfalls until his brain was spinning wildly. Unlike so many hitmen from the realms of fiction and the big screen, he had no military background and was quite unsuited to becoming a sniper and taking out his target from a distance, even if he was provided access through the Bureau to the necessary hardware, and his eyesight had been sharper than it now was. Which only left the alternative of completing the task at close quarters again, a prospect he didn't relish but came to realise was going to become his future burden in life, or should that have been in death?

The person he had been tasked to eliminate was a man in his early 40s, who actually happened to live a close distance from where Leonard was himself situated, a stone's throw from both Astor Place and St Mark's.

Had they inadvertently crossed paths on the street, in a store in recent weeks? Life was, as he knew, so full of curious coincidences. At any rate, it would make any preliminary surveillance easier to set up; no late nights skulking around the New Jersey shore or travelling afar. He would be able to sleep in his own bed every night while he collected the information, deciphered the man's patterns and habits, instead of haunting the bleakness of airport departure lounges or identikit chain hotel rooms. Not that he felt he was entitled to any joy or illusory sunlight in the commerce of death!

The apartment building stood twelve storeys high, overdue in exterior maintenance, its façade in need of a good clean-up and it did not have a doorman. Donning a knitted beanie, an old denim jacket, a washed-out grey sweatshirt and a pair of cargo pants he'd picked up at a Goodwill store and carrying a re-sealed but now empty Amazon delivery box, he ventured into the building's exiguous foyer in the guise of a delivery man to get a feel for the place. Two parallel rows of rusting metal letter boxes covered the left-hand wall that led to a set of dark stairs and the elevator. Few of the post boxes had names, just apartment numbers. He cast a rapid glance around but ventured no further into the building and beat a swift retreat before he could be seen by any arriving or leaving residents. There was in truth little to learn from the exercise, but Leonard knew that the meticulous gathering of seemingly unimportant information was indispensable to the stalking process. You never knew what element would possibly come into play when it came to the crucial part of the assignment so you had to work the odds. Later, back at his own place, he jotted down some notes and then studiously memorised them before disposing of the crumpled page. He'd learned early on not rely on his laptop in his line of work. He purged his viewing history like clockwork every night before going to bed until it became a second habit, even when he had not used it whether casually or nefariously.

He woke early the following morning and kept a watch on the building but the target failed to make an appearance before midday and only then to visit the nearby Walgreen's where he stocked up on soda water and aspirin before returning to his own apartment. After a few days of sheltering under a convenient bodega awning, Leonard came to the conclusion that the man didn't appear to have a fixed job or regular hours. This made any precise planning or making an informed choice as to the method he would use to dispose of him much more difficult. For someone who had come to be a hitman almost accidentally, or at any rate involuntarily, Leonard was surprised at how seriously he was beginning to take its minutiae. Although, he reasoned, it was also a question of survival.

But then, what else was there to do, but count the days leading to nowhere and dreading the dreams that every night brought? Nightmares, circular hauntings that made no sense and that even Freud himself would have had difficulty interpreting, leaving him every single morning in a state of wakefulness that found him even more exhausted already than he had been when sleep had drawn him inside its welcome refuge the previous night.

Following four days of non-stop surveillance on the target,

he needed a break. All of a sudden, he felt a sense of longing taking hold of his much-compromised soul. But for what? Long ago, before his life had turned to shit, it was a feeling that was sadly familiar. A longing in the depths of his heart and the pit of his stomach, for something someone. Nearly always a woman. One he knew or, more often, one he wanted to know better and had no illusion she would ever reciprocate.

He showered, shaved, bought himself a garlic bagel at the nearby store on 6th close to the indie movie house and then took the direction to Tribeca.

It had been several weeks since he'd been to Wanda's.

He found it shuttered. No sign in the window indicating why.

Normally at this time of morning, it would have been open and busy, serving breakfast to the regulars and passers-by attracted by the smells of coffee and food.

He stood there wondering.

Around 10.30 am the adjacent store which sold overpriced gadgets and knick knacks opened. He enquired about Wanda's.

'It's closed down,' he was informed.

'How come?'

'One day she just didn't open.'

'When?'

'Two weeks ago, I think. Came out of the blue.'

Where had all the regulars migrated to, he wondered?

'Does anyone know why?'

'We have the same landlord. Even he hasn't a clue. Says that if he has no further news, he might repossess the premises next month. Seems the rent is paid until the end of the month, and then he can take some form of action.'

'The place was always busy. It doesn't make sense it could have gone out of business …'

'I know. And a prime location. I'm sure they'll find someone overnight to take it over.'

Through the window, the café looked like a room full of ghosts, the tables sitting all pretty in a row, the chairs piled up in each corner, the floor gleaming in the reflection of the morning light as if it had been washed just minutes ago, the counter metal bright. But no living soul animating its emptiness.

He had briefly known some of them, even their names. It was typical of the way life threw things at you when you least expected it and you would then spend an eternity asking yourself whatever happened to so and so? Wanda? Kris? Georgia and her child?

But then, there were those he remembered. The lost ones. All women, of course. If he pictured himself mentally as the hero of his own paperback novel, they were invariably the stars of the movie adaptations that never reached the greenlight stage; scripts both real and evanescent, dreams floating in the wind, fragments of what could have been.

Many years ago, when he still thought of himself as a writer, during a fortnight's holiday in the Maldives, he'd penned a short novel in part inspired by THE STORY OF O in which the abecedary of BDSM was transformed by the then emerging Internet. Sales proved average, but a well-known Hollywood actress, whose backside in nude scenes he had long lusted after, had surprisingly acquired the film rights for a handsome sum, although the project never went into production. He was left with various editions of the book on his shelves, in diverse languages, all proclaiming 'soon to be a major motion picture' and with the money safely in the bank.

The story was about the travails of a married woman in Montreal whose life felt hollow and incomplete, who initially began trawling hotel bars near the airport in search of nameless hook-ups. He somehow associated this with vague and distorted memories of the movie that David Cronenberg made of CRASH. Still yearning for more, the woman would eventually move on to more dangerous assignments of an extreme BDSM nature through anonymous contacts she would make online. The tale unfolded through her email correspondence with a writer who lived in London who never either met her or even found out what she looked like. The Internet handle she hid behind was 'Montana', after the American state.

Time passed and he found himself yet again trawling through the dark world that lurked ever invitingly behind his computer screen and came across a fetish website which piqued his curiosity. Skipping at random between successive links and revealing photographs he came across a site member who called herself 'State of Montana' and allegedly lived in Antarctica (as all regulars of the site who preferred to remain partly anonymous did) and listed her age and gender as 100F, in a further attempt at protecting her identity. She stated she was a submissive in search of a master, according to her profile and mission statement. She regularly posted artful photographs of herself, almost always in black and white. She claimed to be heteroflexible, a definition he hadn't come across before. A leg coated in pale, alabaster skin which through the miracles of perspective appeared endless; her pierced nipples; the intimate geography of her shapely perfect-sized breasts; her lips; the curve of her arse. Day by day, he mentally juggled all the photos she had posted and attempted to reconstitute the jigsaw puzzle of her appearance, but there were always pieces missing and there was no way of knowing the whole of her. Her hair was blonde and unruly in an artful way, her corsets and lingerie lacy looked expensive, and the collection of self-taken images all appeared to have been shot in a kitchen. Her classy shoes always had towering heels but somehow he could never fit all the parts together, missing a shoulder, her eyes, her genitalia (which she never revealed fully and always hid behind thin-fingered hands cupping her intimacy) and other elusive territories plucked from her private landscape. He reckoned a lot of other men around the world were also following her, similarly proving incapable of recreating her true portrait.

She was the character from his book miraculously brought to life.

A woman he had created on the page who had now emerged into the world as a real person.

The fact she called herself Montana and quoted the title of his novel was too much of a coincidence. She must have read his book.

Leonard was torn: should he send her a private message and reveal he was the man who wrote this book that now appeared to mean so much to her? Should he confess that her photos not only intrigued him but made him swell with desire? How can you communicate with a phantom?

He was acquainted with someone who had conquered the more arcane art of computing but also knew how to navigate the secret shores of the dark web. Through him he managed to obtain her IP and they narrowed her location down to Norway. Nothing more precise.

He messaged her. Questioning her about her handle's connection to the novel, but not revealing he was its author. She replied in the affirmative, signing off as 'Anna'.

Later that same morning, she disappeared from the notorious fetish website and all the wonderful photographs she had posted, beautiful exhibitionist that she was, had been deleted.

Leonard was bereft.

Sorry for himself that he had somehow not thought of downloading all the enticing and provocative images she had dispersed across her page on the site, although he guessed, accurately, this would not have proven technically possible.

In his novel, Montana had also faded away, never to be heard of again. Another ghost in the folds of the Internet, leaving only bittersweet memories in her wake.

The following day, he was sorely tempted to book a one-way flight to Oslo. He had no clue what he would do after landing at Gardermoen. Maybe Anna lived in Bergen, Stavanger or Trondheim? Like Montana, she might be married and just indulging her exhibitionist streak and not a deeper need. He didn't even speak a word of Norwegian.

But he never did. Cowardice? He was at the stage of his life where the longing was not yet strong enough to throw the dice in the faint hope it would fall flat with right number on display.

And Anna became yet another memory, a sentimental nostalgia.

He had two choices: somehow force his way into the mark's apartment and do the deed there, in the knowledge he normally lived alone, or take the risk of making the hit outside, factoring in the prospect of being seen or caught on CCTV, let alone causing unforeseen collateral damage.

Leonard weighed the options at his disposal.

Another morning of waiting outside the target's apartment, buffeted by a bitter wind winding its way down the Avenues, up early in case he changed his habit, but again the guy didn't emerge until close to midday. But he was dressed differently on this occasion. Less informal than on previous surveillance shifts. He wore a pair of black trousers, dress shoes, a white button-down Oxford shirt and a grey jacket. Holding an attaché case. With a three or four day beard, speckled with grey, and his hair swept back. His version of casual chic. Off on business?

He paused as he swept through the apartment building's heavy door, as if hesitant to venture onto the street and Leonard thought for a moment that he was just standing there in deep contemplation maybe waiting for a Uber he might have ordered or someone on his way to pick him up. Or possibly trying to decide whether it was cold enough to retrace his steps and go fetch a coat. He appeared to take a deep breath and finally stepped forward. Got into his stride, legs now in motion and made his way west, crossing Astor Place and progressing to Broadway, then straight across and heading for Washington Square Park, almost in the direction Leonard had initially come from. He passed the Park, eyes looking straight ahead as he hurried past the bank of expensive brownstones that bordered Washington Square and then reached Waverly Place. For a brief moment Leonard speculated that the guy was planning to meet someone for a late breakfast or the bar of the boutique hotel that stood on the corner or hoping to catch a yellow cab outside the hotel, but he continued all the way to the corner with 6th and took the sheltered steps down into the West 4th Street subway, by the CVS pharmacy that had stood there for decades. As he passed the grey stone steps leading to the art deco lobby of the Washington Square Hotel, Leonard felt a shiver pass through his heart, the memory of a woman he had spent time with here so many years back. Another of his collection of ghosts.

He followed.

Pulled his scarf around his chin and put on a pair on sunglasses. At first glance he couldn't spot any CCTV cameras, but there was no point being careless. A plan was taking seed in his mind, a spur of the moment thing. But it could work, he reckoned. In some cases, the instructions from the Bureau made it clear that the hit had to be seen as a killing, an assassination. A message to others, a clear and open warning. But most of the times, this was not compulsory: an accident was as good as an open hit. On this occasion, his instructions had given him carte blanche. As long as the man ended up dead, whoever had commissioned the hit would be satisfied. There was no message being sent to third parties unknown.

Down the stained concrete stairs the man he was shadowing moved, oblivious to his close follower. The rank smells of the New York subway rose as they descended, sweat, dampness, urine, stale tobacco.

They reached the platform where a D train was moving out on the right-hand track, an Express destined for Coney Island, its orange marker flying by. More memories piercing the surface of Leonard's mind, a messy killing the previous year he was hoping to forget. Uneasy as he had been seeing the dead man's eyes staring at him at death, a look of surprise or resignation until his consciousness faded fully.

It was between rush hours, the commuting crowds now

safely ensconced in their offices or places of work and the lunching folk still to emerge. The platforms were sparsely populated.

The muted roar of the tunnels rose and fell and people moved along and shuffled on both sides like pieces on a chess board with a logic of their own. Leonard never let the man out of his sight as he shadowed him closely. Now, he stood motionless, waiting for his train, arms by his side, one hand grasping the handle of his attaché case, relaxed, indifferent to his surroundings, unaware he was being closely observed.

Another train filed into the station but he kept on standing still; not the line he was waiting for.

Inch by inch, Leonard shuffled closer to him, holding his breath, with an eye on the tunnel, now waiting for the faint flash of light and rumbling vibration that would indicate the next train was approaching. The C line.

The man twitched in readiness, and moved half an inch forward in anticipation; to his right, a young woman in jogging gear, wearing headphones, took two steps away, positioning herself in relation to where the door of the subway carriage would open. This allowed Leonard to silently move into her space. The sound of the nearing train grew louder. He was now almost touching the man in the grey jacket he had been following. He took a deep breath as the dim circle of light grew larger in the mouth of the tunnel, the train steadily approaching the station. He was now shoulder to shoulder with his mark, could smell his pungent aftershave or was it the lotion he had liberally used to slick his hair back?

The train's incoming vibrations were edging closer and closer.

It finally emerged from the maw of the tunnel.

Leonard waited. Patiently. Calculating the distance, the train's diminishing speed, the right moment to pounce.

Now.

There was a rush of warm, fetid air displaced by the advancing train as it rushed out of the narrow tunnel,

He gave a sudden shove into the man's back, while

tripping him with his right foot so he would lose his balance. For an instant everything seemed to freeze, like a celluloid movie trapped inside its projector. The train, the platform, the lights, the man realising he could no longer avoid falling forward. Then, as if a switch had been activated, matters accelerated. The stranger toppled over, letting go of his attaché case as panic took a hold of him and the front of the incoming train surged forward, unstoppable, inevitable. He didn't even scream. There was no time for it as the realization of what was unfolding came too fast and furiously. Leonard instinctively took a step back, already distancing himself from the point of impact.

The sound of the body colliding with the metal wall of the train was surprisingly discreet, a small impact thud.

The jogger nearby screamed.

Leonard retreated slowly.

The attention of the other bystanders on the platform was drawn to the accident and they all rushed towards the scene as he stepped back and rather than make his way to the stairs and reach for the street, improvised, taking advantage of the fact another train was arriving on the opposing tracks to board it and leave the scene of the crime while the crowds in the station were still trying to make sense of what had just happened and ignored him altogether.

An hour later, he was on the phone to the Bureau.

'It's done.'

'Excellent. Payment will be authorised within the hour.'

They were always meticulously professional: the money was in his offshore account in a matter of minutes.

Rushing past the steps of the Washington Square Hotel the previous week had opened floodgates he had hoped to keep locked. From before he had inadvertently become a killer, when he had another life.

Once again, he was facing empty days, sitting in his apartment trying to shield himself from bittersweet memories.

A familiar face came into focus in his mind.

Giulia in Manhattan, pinned down in the canyons between the Avenues where the wind blows hard, peering towards the sky that lurks above the skyscrapers, the uncountable high rises that dominate her present horizon.

Leonard, her married lover is away at a meeting and she wanders up 6th waiting for him to become free.

Later they will return to the hotel where they will fuck again in the small room overlooking Washington Square until they are both dripping with sweat and sore from the friction between their parts, but ready for more the moment they cease, on the bed, on the floor, in the bathtub.

They will kiss, argue, embrace, fight. She wants him as her own and resents the fact he belongs to another woman and sometimes has to phone home while she retreats to the bar by the hotel lobby when he does so. She wants a boyfriend she can meet whenever she wishes, to share a coffee with, to debate books and politics, to laugh along with. Her married lover seldom laughs, as his mind is not always completely there.

He had a reading the other night in a subterranean club near the Bowery and she was jealous because she knew the story he was reading from, accompanied by a melancholy Nick Cave and Warren Ellis soundtrack, the CD of which he had brought along and carefully timed to accompany his words, had been inspired by a woman whom he knew before her. She wondered whether one day he would write books about her. He did. Three novels and a handful of short stories, but by then they were no longer together because she had reluctantly called a halt to their relationship. She knew she was breaking his heart even though he agreed it was best in view of their age difference. Both were realistically all too aware they had no possible future together

She had arrived in New York a day late, having misplaced her passport the morning before while having a coffee and some pastry at a bar in Barcelona airport and missed her flight, until it was located and she was rescheduled to travel 24 hours later. She had called him in tears with news of the delay.

He was the first man she had properly slept with. Fucked. And quickly realised in his arms that she enjoyed the act of fucking. It was all she had expected and more.

Six months later both back in Europe, he came to visit her in Rome and they had enjoyed an illicit weekend in a hotel a half hour away from the city, where they stood out as, he reckoned, the archetypal May to September couple among the few other guests, the older man with the younger girl. But they had no care what onlookers thought. She drove him back to the airport and they both knew this was the last time they would see each other. It was for their own good, but it still hurt.

She would block him from her Facebook page and somehow disappeared altogether from the Net, despite her journalistic career taking off. She must have arranged it that way to fool the search machines, but then she had always been more fluent with technology than him, probably something to do with the generational gap.

She disappeared from his life like a character from a Murakami novel who ventures into the jungle in search of untold, enigmatic dreams and personal cravings and is obliterated from the surface of the planet.

She had wild curly hair, her breasts were small and ever so delicate to the probing touch of his fingers and his mouth, her dark pubic hair was untrimmed, a gate to a box of treasures and a light brown stain the shape of Sicily spread across the skin of her inner right thigh; she joked she was a fervent communist and she enjoyed wearing vintage clothes.

They made love in a ski resort in the Alps while a song by Pink Floyd played on her computer as they coupled and he had an epiphany that she would be the last great love of his life right as he penetrated her for the first time and was overcome by the warmth of her body encircling him inside and outside. They made love in the medieval village of Calcata, a half hour north of Rome, in London, in New York, Barcelona and a beach resort to its south and on that final occasion by a lake in Italy close to the castle where George Clooney or some other celebrity had married.

He had always promised to take her to New Orleans and long wondered if it would have changed her mind.

And now she was a ghost, living only in his memory. More prosaically, she was probably now married with kids, partnered with somebody nearer her own age, no longer an avowed communist and freelancing for Italian newspapers and radio. But, in his previous life, a man not unlike him had written the books and stories about her, in which she appeared as in a hall of mirrors, none of them telling the actual truth about their relationship, skirting it, improvising it, narrating what had happened and what might have happened. It was all he could do. It was all he then knew how to do, turning the grief into words.

Until the words had ran out.

Leonard kills again.

The Bureau send him overseas.

The woman is staying at a resort in Phuket. She is not alone. The man she is with appears to be her husband. Or possibly her lover. Their conversations at dinner in the open-air restaurant are limited, as if they've known each other for a long time and have run out of topics to discuss. Leonard observes them just a few tables away. It was arranged for his room to be on the same block as theirs, his adjacent balcony overlooking one of the pools. Sitting there at dawn, he watches the ocean awaken as the sun rises over the horizon. The hotel is separated from the beach by just a narrow road designed for joggers or bicycles. A flag is planted in the sand. Pink. Suggesting swimmers should take care when out at sea. By mid-afternoon, the flag's colour might have switched to red as the waves usually increase in size as the day progresses. But it's not a surfing beach; those are further down the coast. Here, the danger was the highly treacherous undertow.

He watches.

He observes.

Notes patterns, habits.

Waiting for the right occasion.

He has learned to be patient.

The resort's meagre bookshelf consists of airport paperbacks left by previous visitors, crumpled copies, water-stained pages, identikit romances and thrillers that have no appeal to him. But he reads, sitting on his lounger on the opposing side of the pool, sipping cold sodas, one eye on his prey. Her companion is dozing while she is listening to something -music or podcast- on her iPods. On occasion, she steps over to the pool and immerses herself to the waist. Never swims. She has thick ankles and, he guesses, her breasts and face have benefited from corrective surgery at some stage. She must be in early 50s, but dresses and displays herself like a younger woman, with a faint touch of bravado and insouciance.

The day lingers on.

By now, the sun is lower and the sky and the heat more tolerable. Her male half has come back to life and makes regular visits to the poolside bar to replenish their glasses, but aside from that Leonard doesn't observe much in the way of communication between the pair. They seem bored or studiously indifferent to each other. Married, then.

The man rises from his lounger and pulls up his towel. They briefly speak. She nods. He moves away from the pool in the direction of their ground floor room. She remains in place. Half an hour later, the man hasn't reappeared and Leonard watches her lazily stretch out her limbs and then slide off the chair and after a moment's deliberation, taking note of the fact the pool is crowded with tourists and teenagers, she ambles towards the bar and moves beyond it to the fence separating the resort from the beach that lies on the other side of the narrow dirt road. Leonard quickly gets up and, never keeping her out of sight though safely distant, follows her. Either she is going to swim or just planning to browse at some of the improvised stalls selling sunglasses and local fabrics lined up around the beach's entrance.

She ignores the street sellers and treads her way onto the sand.

Yards behind, Leonard follows her onto the sand. It's damn hot and he is barefoot, while the woman he is shadowing is wearing crocs. He bites his lip to neuter the pain, knowing he can't turn back and lose a possible opportunity.

She gingerly sets a foot and then the other in the water. Thirty or so yards behind her, the sand he is now walking on is cooler, its sting muted by the nearness of the sea and the wavelets that have washed over it back and forth as they break over the incoming shoreline.

As he tiptoes into the Andaman Sea, ahead of him the clear blue water has reached her waist.

He takes a deep breath, and plunges forward, swimming towards the woman. She stands there, vicariously offering her flank to the rush of the incoming waves, taking pleasure in the way the water embraces her, droplets pearling off her body, hair wet and streaming down her back, her balance increasingly unsteady.

Leonard swims under the wall of continuous waves, emerging for breath and checking her position while quickly scanning the horizon for the presence of other bathers. They are few. Far apart. Oblivious to him and the woman.

He takes in as much air in his lungs as he can and pivots towards her, eyes initially closed. Reaches her. Still under the surface, he strikes the back of left knee. She loses her balance, surprised by the unexpected underwater contact. She stumbles. He rises out of the water and taking advantage of her surprise and unsteadiness, firmly grabs a hold of her hair and pulls her head below the surface of the sea before she can fully scream. The waves surrounding them give out a mighty roar that swallows her feeble cry for help.

He holds her down in the water now. All the time fighting the lower current coursing around his ankles, the undertow pulling him back; she writhes in place, torn between his strength and the pull of the tide. He doesn't let go. Her whole body shudders. Fear. Graduating to terror as the air in her lungs begs to be released. He pulls harder, her head fully submerged, trembling, terrified.

It feels to Leonard as if he is struggling both with the woman and the contrary pull of the ocean trying to lure him backwards, to dislodge him from his position. Her movements weaken. Now just a shudder. Her hands no longer windmilling in the water in her panic. Her will now broken. Her arms float by her side.

Finally, she is motionless.

But he keeps a firm hold on her for a minute longer until he is certain she has perished.

At last, he lets go. Her body like a blanket shimmering below the surface, her eyes bulging, her mouth open in an ugly rictus.

Not a killing he has enjoyed.

He detests when he has to do the deed at close quarters, but knows he is not trained in long distance hits, not a sniper who manages to keep his hands clean.

It will look like a drowning. Her lifeless body washed out to sea carried by the tides.

He struggles back to the shore, his weakening legs fighting the heavy undertow, the enormous waves battering his back. Progress is slow and painful but he finally reaches the waterline and steps, stumbling, partly out of breath onto the beach.

The sun is beginning to set, an orange orb like a ripe peach in the immeasurable distance.

He briefly wonders as he enters the resort's grounds where or when, if ever, the sea will throw up the woman's body. At some distant spot down the long coast or maybe by the stone monument to the victims of the tsunami that stands a mile or so away closer to the actual town?

But Leonard is soon thinking of the long flight back home.

But is Manhattan home?

Or has it by default become somewhere to count down the slow days to his own death?

How had it all begun?

Leonard knew the answer.

He could no longer bear the grief of living in the house his wife and he had shared. Unable to dispose of her clothes, her jewellery, trapped in a space she created. A burden of grief and guilt. He had been an imperfect husband. He had been unfaithful on several occasions over the years, a mere man living in a world of women, unable to resist the tides of reciprocal desire. Which in no way meant he hadn't loved her. Or the others he had been with.

On one occasion, he had even been close to jettisoning his marriage. That close. But something had happened which he had no control over.

He thought she knew, but she remained silent.

Her name was Kate.

It stood for Kathryn.

Her backside was a thing of beauty, and reminded him of Nicole Kidman's in EYES WIDE SHUT. Pale and firm, standing between a thin waist and sturdy legs. She walked with long, manly strides and the way it moved, whether unveiled or closely espousing her form beneath pencil or billowing skirts, made it impossible for him to look away, turning his raging desire into something priapic.

They were introduced to each other at a conference in the Midlands but had no professional excuses to keep in touch thereafter, even more so as he had inadvertently given a smattering of bad reviews to several books she had acquired and published.

But he couldn't in the following weeks get her out of his mind.

He was a subscriber to a high-end luxurious literary magazine devoted to erotica, which featured both short stories and fine art photography. In the then current issue, there was a black and white portfolio of images by an American photographer who was also known as a poet and the model, whose face was never seen in the photos, reminded him of Kate Callaghan, although at this stage he could only guess at the form of her body. He couldn't avoid masturbating over the images of this white, lanky and languorous geography of naked flesh sprawled over sofas and sand, her face always out of shot, but belonging to Kate in his imagination. He had a complicated relationship with pornography despite his own sensible public persona.

The feelings kept on stirring inside him, daily coming to the boil and he finally gave up and wrote her a letter, which he posted to her office, in which he casually confirmed how pleasant it had been to meet in Nottingham and maybe they could meet again for a drink or a bite one day to discuss the art of crime writing – the only thing they so far had in common. He ended the short letter, signing off 'respectfully but lustfully'. It caught her attention.

She was married, of course. But so was Leonard

Some years before, he had been one of the first critics to review JG Ballard's CRASH in NEW SCIENTIST magazine, of all places, where he was sometimes indulged and allowed to review left of field titles. He had described the novel as one of the first instances where sex and technology intermingled and his quote was picked up for years on the book's successive British paperback editions. At a private BAFTA preview of the Cronenberg screen adaptation, which Ballard attended, he was captivated by the face (and body) of the Canadian actress Kara Unger (before she changed her name to Deborah Kara Unger) and was also reminded of her when he met Kate. The sensual convergence between Kate and Nicole Kidman's arses manifested itself later, of course, once he had acquired carnal knowledge of the exquisite posterior in question.

They did meet for a drink; an evening of silences and hesitations and personal confessions in a West End pub. It was all he could do not to touch her knee or lean over for a kiss.

She then had to travel home and catch her train at Charing Cross Station. He volunteered to drive her there although it was only a ten-minute walk away. His car was parked in the large underground Chinatown car park. He was driving up the steep ramp to the car park's exit, his hand on the handbrake, the silence between them thunderous when, out of the blue, she laid her hand on his and he knew they would come together.

A week later they had made the necessary arrangements and driven to a hotel by Heathrow airport, where they hoped none of their common acquaintances were likely to see them book in for the day. He had brought along strawberries and a bottle of white wine.

Following their initial frantic couplings – it was all they had both expected, feverish, desperate, rough, releasing days and months of frustration and desire – as they relaxed between the sweaty bedsheets, he fed her the fruit while she sipped the wine. Later, in jest, he crushed the remaining strawberries and spread their mush across her lips, coloured her pale pink nipples with a brush of scarlet and, encouraged by her passive acceptance of his kink, painted her outer labia red. Now, she was truly an Amazon.

Another affair he would one day, after the bitter conclusion when she, in extremis, decided to remain with her husband, write stories about which she never forgave him for.

Kate, Anna, Giulia.

More than just names: the women who unwittingly had made him the man he now had become.

A man who loved women and waited in a Manhattan room for the phone to ring.

A killer for hire.

10
Dance Me To the End of Love

He was in the habit of picking up his free copy of the Village Voice most Thursdays from the rusting dispensers on the corner of Mercer and Houston. He seldom read the features or news items, mostly restricting himself to the film and music reviews, and had left the previous week's copy on his sofa spread open at a random page. Returning one afternoon from shopping for essentials at the Morton Williams supermarket on La Guardia and Bleecker, about to drop his bag in the kitchen area, he caught a small headline from the corner of his eye.

NOTORIOUS DANCE HALL TO CLOSE DOWN.

The only dance hall he could think of in New York was the Continental. There were others, he knew, but none sprang to mind.

He unloaded the bottles and food in the fridge, shook off his jacket and made a beeline for the abandoned newspaper and took a closer look at the feature.

It appeared the Continental had lost its liquor license following a lengthy investigation by local authorities into a series of both financial irregularities and unconfirmed suspicions of drug-related activities on the premises. The article also hinted at possible instances of human trafficking and prostitution. None of this came as a surprise to Leonard. The establishment was scheduled to close its doors at the end of the following week and its management had declared they were hoping to go out with a bang, with a spectacular 48-hour dance-a-thon the likes of which, they stated, the city had not seen since the roaring 30s.

Leonard smiled.

It was like another door leading back to his past was being closed for good.

Although he knew it didn't make sense, he intuited already he would visit the place one final time. Curiosity? A morbid sense of attraction? It was drawing him back, not so much to provide answers but so that he could immerse himself again in its seductive atmosphere, the smells, the lights, the unfolding spectacle of characters at the end of their tether bathing in its fetid waters. His sort of environment, casting its rules of attraction far and wide and appealing to parts of him he wouldn't openly acknowledge publicly. The wrong parts.

He tried to remember Helen's face, but her features kept blurring, the contour of her lips in constant motion, as if hidden by a cloud moving across her pale skin, details shifting, never quite properly pinned down. Even the recalled shape of her body couldn't be fixed in hypothetical amber with any precision. Or the actual colour of her eyes.

He would go to the Continental tonight, Leonard decided.

The dance floor was crowded and there were queues at the bar, but the atmosphere had a ghoulish end of times quality to it. Lighting intermittent and patchy, flickering, throwing unhealthy shadows across stressed faces and grey flesh. There was barely a couple of handfuls of taxi dancers scouting the perimeter in search of willing, paying partners, their outfits similarly colourless and dull. The orchestra, if there was going to be one tonight, hadn't yet taken to the stage and piped heavy rock music poured out of loudspeakers dotted around the cavernous room at shoulder height, the insistent thud of the bass notes turned up high.

He vaguely recognised one of the dancers. An ageing redhead with an asymmetric bob who had been around when he had first begun to frequent the Continental what felt like an eternity ago. Her threadbare dress had echoes of 1930s flapper fashion, the sort of garment the likes of Daisy Buchanan and her merry cohorts would have worn in THE GREAT GATSBY.

She caught his eyes and nodded in recognition.

He nodded back.

'So what's the story?' he asked, 'the grand finale dance-a-thon?'

'Ah, that … It begins at midnight. Will last a whole 48 hours and then they close the doors for good and I have to find myself another gig. Will likely go back to waitressing, I think, not that I'm looking forward to it … So, where do I know you from? You're not a regular.'

'I used to come here, but that was a long while ago.'

'That's what I thought. I've been here that long, too. Almost become part of the furniture. The place sure is a touch sleazy, but I've liked being here. I've had to work my ass off in worse places, although that wooden dance floor has been hell on shoe rubber. Had to get myself new pumps like clockwork every single month! And I've seen so many girls come and go, I can tell you …'

Leonard guessed he had already asked her about Helen on a previous occasion, so didn't enquire again. In truth, it was a problem he had by now given up hope ever solving.

He smiled wryly. 'A pity it's closing down, though. The Continental has its charm.'

'Damn right you are. The stories I could tell. Someone should maybe write a book one day about the wild nights of ye good old Continental!'

'Perhaps someone will: some anonymous punter might have been taking studious notes between dances and might one day birth the chronicles of the Continental?'

The older dancer grinned. 'Well, as long as he or she doesn't name names. Some things are best kept under wraps. What happened here best stay here.' She gave Leonard a knowing wink, as she was approached by a would-be dance partner and moved her attention to the prospect.

The buzz circulating through the room was increasing, a sense of excitement spreading through the hall.

Forcing his way through the incoming tide of new arrivals, Leonard stepped back to the lobby where he treated himself to a can of soda from a dispensing machine and took the stairs to the circular balcony that overlooked the dance floor. He found a table that overlooked the proceedings below and sat himself down, popped the can open, took a sip of the lukewarm drink and began observing the stir of the crowds.

There was a definite sense of expectancy, something in the air, a spread of excitement circulating through the place.

Then, like a switch being pulled, the piped music stopped, leaving an invisible gap in the air.

The orchestra emerged from the side of the stage. A cohort of middle-aged men wearing white jackets and black trousers, scarlet bow ties circling their throats, hair oiled back, carrying their instruments, mostly overweight and suburban-looking, like a band of mob acolytes presiding over a mafia wedding. Any minute now, he guessed, they might even launch into the theme of the Godfather!

They filed onto the proscenium, some with cigarettes dangling negligently from their lips, with a general look of bored resignation, shuffled around, adjusting their positions and, at the signal of the principal trumpet player, finally launched into music. He recognised Duke Ellington's 'Caravan'. Under the glare of unforgiving spotlights, most of the musicians already appeared to be sweating profusely.

Below, the dancers aggregated, coupled up, triggering their ritual of spins, loops and at times geometrical movements as they took possession of the dance floor, brushing past each other in accelerated motion, striving for composure and elegance, puppets to the music, a hand on a shoulder here, grasping a waist there, backs straight, smiles fixed, composing themselves for the hours to come. Some couples effortlessly glided along while others appeared more tentative, too attentive to the way they moved, stiff, almost shy at the thought of letting go and allowing the music to dictate the direction of their flow.

Leonard kept on watching them, detached but fascinated,

like an entomologist observing the hidden patterns of miniscule insects let loose on a new patch of grass. The spectacle amused him; he was mentally already highlighting which couples would last the longest, would still be standing on their feet as the night, and following day, would progress. Which unfortunate souls would collapse and exit the ring when their reserves of energy would become depleted, the sad, inevitable losers in this uncommon arena devoid of lions and gladiators, this Manhattan second-rate version of the Roman Colosseum. But neither was he a betting man or likely to stay for the duration, knowing the ultimate hours of the dance-a-thon would drag on and the whole shebang would become a cemetery of indignities and broken hopes.

His phone rang.

The number was familiar.

The Bureau.

'Hello?'

'There is an urgent job.'

A woman's voice he knew well.

'How urgent?'

'Right now.'

'Really?'

Not only was the assignment uncommon, unlike any he had previously undertaken, but it also meant a total lack of preparation. Unsafe. Risky. Unprofessional.

The orchestra had now segued into an expansive Benny Goodman piece, the brass section in full flow, the drummer marking the beat like an automaton, albeit a skinny one with a pencil-thin moustache who looked more like a gigolo than a musician.

'Yes, tonight.'

'I'm at East 11th Street. Where do you need me to go?'

'We know where you are.' Leonard felt a shudder run down his spine. How could they have located him? 'At the dance hall.'

Once again, the Bureau's tentacles appeared to be worryingly far-reaching. He smiled wryly.

'I'm impressed. Do you have me followed on a permanent basis?'

'Too expensive ...' There was a hint of humour on the other end of the line. 'Let's just say we have our ways ...'

'So, where do you need me to go?'

'Nowhere.'

'I don't get it.'

'Your target is presently in the same building.'

'Oh. How convenient.'

'Isn't it?'

Was this a test of some sorts?

'I have no weapons or any form of equipment with me, though.'

'Then you'll just have to improvise.'

'That's easier said than done.'

'You'll find a way. We have the fullest confidence in your ability to improvise when it comes to the crunch.'

'I'm flattered.'

The woman from the Bureau continued, informing him of the mark's identity. He tried to recall her name; she had told him once. It escaped him. Which easily solved his first problem: it was the drummer in the orchestra.

Leonard had no choice but to accept the assignment, although he was terribly unhappy about the task ahead. It was too close to home for comfort, and his opportunities were limited. The damn guy was on stage for the majority of the time and even during breaks would be backstage in the company of his fellow musicians, which allowed him few opportunities to find himself alone with him. And then there was the lack of weapon. Leonard's mind switched into top gear; his eyes fixed on the dance floor where the competing couples still swirled to the beat of the music in a galaxy of colours like paint being mixed on a palette. Only one possibility sprang to mind: he would have to strangle the man. Not a prospect he relished in the slightest; the drummer appeared wiry but strong and would offer arduous resistance even if he could come up on him by surprise. His arms would have much strength. Leonard was not a particularly physical person. Had never even been in any significant fight even as a child; he was poorly equipped for the new job at hand, he knew, but did not have the option of turning the job down.

'OK,' he finally said and the woman from the Bureau, hearing this, hung up.

From his vantage point sitting on the balcony, he continued to observe the busy dancers and the orchestra in full flow below.

Heat rose towards the ceiling in waves, propelled by the increasingly breathless bodies in eternal motion and their suffocating closeness as they waltzed and boogied the night away, reaching for a still distant destination.

Finally, the band came to a halt, although within seconds the music returned, now blasted through the banks of raised loudspeakers dotting the periphery of the large room. Recorded music, more modern, more frantic, so as to give the competing dancers no respite.

The musicians from the orchestra rose in succession, some wiping their brows, others sighing deeply and they began to file out into the wings.

Leonard descended the stairs, mingling with the milling crowds below, groups of excited spectators, the more formally attired judges of the competition, the long queues of people at the bar taking advantage of the half break. He tried to get his bearings, recalling some of the building's configuration from the occasion a few years back when he had visited the then manager, again prompted by the Bureau and its instructions.

The musicians must have a dressing room, where they could dress, rehearse. He tried to pinpoint where it could be. Naturally, he would not be able to enter it. Do the deed in plain daylight so to speak with the drummer's colleagues in rhythm in attendance, not just potential witnesses but also of necessity obstacles to his murderous intent.

But, he was aware, they would also need toilet breaks. They were human, after all.

He retraced his steps to the lobby and located the short,

narrow corridor leading to the toilets. A crowd of women milled impatiently outside the door to the ladies. And then, he noticed slightly further down the corridor another door which must lead, he estimated, to an area adjacent to the stage. If he was right, the dressing rooms. He gave it a close look. The door could only be opened from stage side. He felt a sigh of relief, his theory proven right: the staff, people working here did not have separate washroom facilities and would need to come through here on their natural breaks.

He began to formulate his plan.

The attack would have to take place much later, in the heart of night when the crowds following the dance-a-thon had shrunk and only the dancers, the musicians and interested parties were still around the building.

He would wait. He was a patient man. He would not leave the premises in search of some sort of weapon. He now knew what he would use. He returned to the balcony, picking up another can of soda and a bottle of Japanese beer from the bar on the way. Although he never drank alcohol. But who was to know?

The music drags on. If the dancers are low on energy, so is the orchestra. The beat is sometimes off, and the brass section solos are lacking in belief, as the musicians eke out yet another big band melody, their faces frozen in a rictus, their movements on the elevated stage bordering on slow motion. It's 2.30 in the morning.

The remaining couples are ambling across the dance floor like puppets controlled by loose strings, uncoordinated, sometimes gasping for breath as if the very act of breathing is proving a supreme effort for survival, their lips dry, their legs aching, their feet screaming blue murder as they shuffle along on automated pilot.

Finally, the song comes to a slow end, its final notes drawn out from the reluctant instruments against their will, and the orchestra once more steps off the stage. Someone is now feeding further music into the loudspeaker as the dancers are allowed no reprieve and continue their repetitive waltz of the damned. Leonard notes it's actually the same mix tape recording that was played during the previous intermission just past midnight. Not that this made any difference to those who had to continue dancing to its strains.

He stations himself in the corridor that leads to the washrooms, an unlit cigarette dangling from his lips as his excuse for loitering, even though he doesn't smoke. In his jacket pocket the beer bottle whose neck he had earlier broken off, concealed, sharp, its serrated edges now catching the fabric of the lining. His right arm dangles against his side in an attempt to conceal the bump the improvised weapon forms.

Folk come and go when, finally, the door leading to the backstage area opens and one of the musicians, the bass player, emerges and makes a beeline for the men's. Leonard catches the door before it automatically closes and quickly jams the lock. Should his initial plan not come to fruition, he now has a fallback and possible access to the orchestra's dressing room. He hopes it won't come to this as he'd much rather there were no witnesses to what he's planning.

He is worried that if he stands in the corridor too long, his presence will be noticed or someone will ask questions.

Time stretches with fewer people visiting the washrooms from either the backstage area or the actual dance hall and Leonard is considering retreating and waiting for the next break in the proceedings. Why did the profession of killing people involve so much waiting, he considered?

About to give up, his nerves on edge, he is taken back when the door to the private area is pushed open and the drummer emerges, almost taking him by surprise as he now no longer expected him. They exchange a furtive glance. Leonard tries to remember whether there was anyone previously left inside the men's washroom, but is uncertain. He'd been making mental notes about the comings and goings, but his attention had strayed.

The man enters the washroom. Leonard takes a deep breath

and follows. His target moves to one of the cubicles while Leonard, never leaving him out of his sight, approaches the wall of urinals.

All the other cubicles, he quickly ascertains, are empty. The two of them are alone in the washroom.

Again, he waits. Blanking out all sounds, the faraway taped music filtering through from the dance floor and the man's grunts behind the cubicle door. He moves to the sinks, watches himself in the mirror above, almost doesn't recognise the man he has become, the tiredness in his features, the lines below his eyes, his sunken cheeks.

He hears the flushing.

His hand moves to the pocket of his jacket.

The drummer emerges from the cubicle, its door swinging behind him as he steps towards the adjacent sink to where Leonard is standing. The musician glances briefly at him as he rolls up his sleeves, failing to recognise him, seeing just another anonymous punter using the facilities. He bends slightly forward as the tap releases the water across his hands.

This was the moment Leonard was waiting for.

He pounces.

Pulls the broken bottle from his pocket and swiftly draws it towards the man's throat, taking him by total surprise. Before his victim can even mutter a single word he violently slashes away at his throat. The broken edge of glass is sharp and penetrates the flesh, cutting deep. Leonard applies further pressure and feels the weapon now reaching bone. The man doesn't have the time to even struggle. The bare echo of a sound makes a vain attempt to pass his lips as his whole body shudders, his hands holding on to the edge of the sink as blood gushes down and mingles with the still pouring water.

Leonard is behind him, still applying all the pressure he can muster but in the mirror that faces them, he can see the abominable panic clouding the man's eyes, as every drop of blood now spurting from his artery splashes against sink and wall and he begins to bear witness to his own death.

Leonard breathes again. In. Out. In.

Pulls his arm back and allows the man's body to crumple down to the floor.

He doesn't rush. Checks for pulse.

None as expected.

There is blood everywhere.

Its metallic smell a sharp reminder of other close kills he'd rather forget.

He had worn gloves. They are soaked and ruined. He will dispose of them later, together with the broken bottle he will tread on repeatedly, shattering it into a hundred pieces before disposing of them down a drain hole on Greenwich Avenue.

He departs the Continental.

He has no concern for the remaining survivors of the dance-a-thon or which sad couple will emerge victorious. Or even whether the sordid festivities will be interrupted when the missing drummer is found and they have to keep on dancing to that same tape on and on, like damned souls in the loop of hell.

He hears a police siren in the distance by the time he reaches Washington Square Park. Even though it's 4 in the morning, there is someone playing the piano under the arch. A small crowd is gathered around her, entranced, curious.

A young woman who reminds him of Kate. Blonde medusa hair, straight posture sitting at the keyboard, grey eyes, slim and long-legged. Like an apparition, a ghost created by the Manhattan night just for his sake.

She is playing a piece of music by Erik Satie.

It's plaintive, heartbreakingly soulful and sad.

But he doesn't linger, just walks on South, ever the professional, and the music slowly fades, its melody lost on the wings of song.

By the time he reaches his apartment, jaywalking across Houston, the night is now empty of sounds.

It takes him hours to find sleep, adrenaline still haunting his veins and he only manages to close his eyes when the rest of New York awakens.

11
What Doesn't Kill You Makes You Crazier

Leonard only learned three days later that the Continental had burned down.

It had taken place in the early hours of the morning of the following day, barely three hours following the assassination.

The incident had unsurprisingly made the front page of the New York Post, not a paper he was in the habit of reading, and he only noticed the headline from a pile of newspapers piled up on the floor by the exit of a local bodega, all bundled up and ready to be returned or disposed of.

He obtained a copy and poured through the limited information provided. There was no mention of a body being found in the washroom. Had it been incinerated in the conflagration? There was speculation that the fire might have been caused by an electrical fault. Leonard thought it was more likely to have been arson and possibly prompted by the likelihood of insurance fraud, in view of the assortment of shady people involved with the Continental. Fortunately, the building's alarm system had been in functioning order and all the dancers, musicians, spectators and staff had been safely evacuated before the fire had spread out of control. There were various photos taken of what remained of the building. It was a total write-off.

He felt a sense of relief combined with one of nostalgia: yet another landmark in his life erased, living now just in memory.

There were so many of these. Just the previous week, he had wandered into Tribeca and seen that the locale where

Wanda's Café had stood was now a store selling novelties or, at any rate, useless designer objects that had held no appeal to him.

Even though he had the feeling that his own life was at a standstill, not moving forward, caught in a form of stasis, the past on the other hand was moving away from him in accelerated motion, leaving him stranded in a curious version of no man's land.

On one hand, he wished badly to hold on to the past, the memories, the faces, the bodies of women still sharp in his mind, the words muttered in the dead of night, the feelings, but on the other all too often they carried an unbearable weight of pain and grief.

He felt he was at some sort of crossroads.

He had calculated he could easily sustain a materially comfortable life in New York on the proceeds of two or three hits a year for the Bureau. His outgoings were modest, his needs limited, and even an eventual fallow period with no jobs would not prove a major inconvenience: he seldom required much in the way of new clothes unless they were necessary for an assignment and later had to be disposed of, had no taste for high-end restaurants and his travel out of town was strictly work-related; he no longer sought vacations in exotic places as, all too often, the locales held too many memories. Yes, it was a dull life but he had resigned himself to the fact it was now his fate. It was too late to change. Routine suited him.

At some stage, reminded of his previous life, Leonard had briefly considered the prospect of a return to writing. The melancholy thought of a desultory homage to Meg, the woman who had circuitously brought him here, changed his itinerary in such a radical manner. The idea of summoning a tale about her life before she knew him. Who she was or had been, why she had become an assassin. It was, briefly, a seductive idea. Had he pursued it, he reckoned he might well have called her Cornelia and narrated her story, her exploits, the way she navigated between good and evil amongst the noir streets of the American dream, highlighting her presence in a nocturnal world straight out of a gallery of Edward Hopper paintings. A character not so much in search of redemption but seeking purpose.

He even desultorily began a chapter but the progress was painful and he eventually gave up, unable to recapture the magic moments where words just flow and a story emerges. Even in better days, he had never truly enjoyed writing, that oppressive feeling of squeezing a story out like blood from stone and the constant doubts clouding his mind. He had been a terribly minor writer, one who moderately enjoyed having written rather than the act of writing itself. Deep down inside, he knew all too well he had no important message to convey to the waiting crowds, no social relevance, was merely a minor division entertainer, delivering crime stories in which everyone predictably died at the end.

So, all things considered, he had given up.

And even though he had hoped to bring Meg back to life again, albeit in the fictional guise of Cornelia, he soon came to the conclusion he was unable to seize her true essence and to persist any further would prove just another betrayal.

Case closed, he reckoned. Let her lie in peace, alongside all the secrets that had coursed through the arc of her life, all to remain in merciful darkness, spared of the indignities his imagination set loose might have inflicted on her.

At least, he owed her that. Dying the way she had was enough punishment, surely?

It had been a whole three months since the last Bureau job.

Leonard had just watched a movie at the Union Square Regal and was walking down Broadway on his way back to his apartment building. He was in no hurry, pondering whether he should eat out or rely on whatever he would find in his fridge. The fall weather was still mild, a gentle breeze streaming past his ears.

'Lennie?'

A woman's voice across the street.

He looked over, unsure she was calling out to him.

She appeared to be in her late 40s, slim, dressed from top to toe in black, a two-piece trouser suit, mannish, a white shirt with frilly cuffs a discreet concession to her gender. Her hair fell to her shoulders, brown, lustrous but streaked with grey highlights. She nodded, confirming it was he she was hailing.

He stood there, motionless as the woman stepped into Broadway between interruptions in the traffic and crossed over towards him.

'Do I know you?'

He had made no friends since his arrival in New York, barely acquaintances, at the defunct dance hall, at the now closed café.

'I know you,' she replied.

'If you did, you'd be aware I don't respond to 'Lennie', or 'Len'. It's just Leonard.'

'Hello Leonard,' she smiled.

He gazed down at her, still trying to place her. Had they previously crossed paths here in Manhattan? Somewhere in Europe?

Something in the tone of her voice held an element of familiarity.

She held his stare, as if hoping he'd puzzle things out.

Then it came to him. Over the phone. When the Bureau had initially made contact with him.

Yes. It was her voice.

'You're with them?' he didn't want to mention the name in public.

'Indeed,' she confirmed. 'Very good.'

'Well, this is unexpected,' Leonard admitted.

'Coffee?' she suggested.

'Why not?'

They both looked around. There was a diner nearby, on the corner of Broadway and 9th Street.

They found a table in a corner where no one could overhear them, watching each other with amusement and curiosity.

'I thought the rules insisted we never meet face to face?' he reminded her.

'If there are rules, there can also be exceptions to them, no?'

'I suppose so … After all, you're the ones who made the rules. I just follow them.'

'And you've done so excellently, I must say.'

'Pleased you think so.'

'I must confess I was unsure of your suitability after the fiasco with the lovely Megan …'

'Why a fiasco? The guy was disposed of, albeit maybe not the way it had been planned.'

'It was messy. And the rules were broken.'

'Ah, those sacred rules again …'

'Anyway, that is now a long time ago, water under the bridge and all that,' the woman said.

'I haven't forgotten. What you did to … Meg … It was cruel and unnecessary,' he countered.

'It was unfortunate, I agree. But it was a majority decision, not just mine.'

'Is that meant to make me feel happier about it all?'

'I'm merely just stating the facts of the case.'

He took a sip of soda. The tall glass was full of ice. He'd forgotten to ask the waitress to hold back on it. The sugary taste of the cola was heavily diluted and bland. The woman now facing him across the table ordered a cappuccino.

'So, I seem to recall you having a name, but it's gone from my memory. Was such a long time ago. Are you willing to reveal it again or does that also go against the rules?'

'It's Ramona,' she revealed.

'Ramona, Ramona, yes, that's it.' Leonard weighed the name on his tongue, trying to get the measure of it. Somehow, the name and the face didn't fit together the way he had expected. But then, what does a Ramona look like or, for that matter, how do names and appearance conjugate?

'So, how long have you worked 'there'?' He felt it wiser not to utter the name of the organisation in public, even though their corner of the diner was empty, between hours, no one around to overhear their conversation.

'Too long,' she replied. 'I actually joined as an accountant, can you believe? Things happened ...'

Leonard had a wry smile 'So we both became accidental killers, so to speak?'

'Seems that way ...'

'Why this meeting?'

Ramona lowered her eyes, a touch of hesitancy. Then looked back at him. 'I'm not sure. I was curious. When the decision was taken to try and recruit you into the fold, I was dubious. Didn't think it would work. That you would comply. But we were all surprised at the way you adapted to the new role. You turned out to be one of the best operatives we've had for ages ...'

'Should I take that as a compliment?'

'I've always wondered why. Closely followed your 'career'. Speculating what in your mental make-up predisposed you to being such an efficient killer. Surely not a lack of empathy, as I've read some of those stories you wrote? So, I was curious, thought that before I leave the scene I wanted to meet you briefly.'

Leonard was pensive. It was a question he had also given much thought to over the course of the past years.

'The jobs gave me a purpose,' he said, after a long interruption.

'I see.' She didn't ask him to elaborate.

'You said you were leaving? How come?'

'Let's just say I've lost my own purpose. Time to retire.'

'I didn't realise it was something one could retire from.' He remembered Meg, and Hopley, the man who had been assigned to train him and had then disappeared.

The diner was filling as the dinner hour neared. A new waitress had come on shift and was hovering around their table, asked them if they wanted another set of drinks or maybe might wish to eat.

Leonard ordered Italian meatballs, while Ramona opted for

the soup of the day. The next hour went by mostly in silence, as if they had no longer much to say to each other but furtive glances worth a thousand words, actual conversation exhausted or unnecessary.

At one stage, he asked Ramona about the man they had initially assigned to him.

'His name was Hopley,' Ramona wistfully said. 'He was a good man.'

'Was?'

She sighed. 'Yes. He fell in love with the wrong person. Lost his way.'

'I liked him.'

'So did I,' and then she fell silent again, no doubt struggling with memories unknown.

He had some questions of his own about the Bureau and the way it functioned, who ran it, owned it, but Ramona made it clear she wouldn't answer.

'So what does retirement hold?' he finally asked her. 'Tropical beach, around the world cruise or just a life of contemplation?'

'Well, I'm not about to write my memoirs,' she chuckled. 'In truth, I don't know ...' she looked away.

'Do they know yet?'

'No.'

'Will they let you go?'

'Probably not.'

'So you'll be going ... on the run?'

'My bags are already packed, arrangements made,' Ramona told him. 'I wanted you to be my last port of call. I had to satisfy my curiosity before I went, actually meet this curious man in the flesh, the one who defied the odds and made a go of an accidental second life. Maybe as a way of kidding myself I might be able do the same, although I assure you I have no plans to kill anyone ... It's definitely not one of my few talents. I told you I was an accountant by training!'

'They're just jobs,' Leonard remarked. 'You gave the orders, I followed them ...'

'That's one way of looking at it.'

A winter darkness was wrapping lower Manhattan in its folds, a starless and cloudless sky.

They parted outside the diner. Wished each other luck with whatever the future held and went their own way. The night swallowed them, he south towards the Village, she north to Uptown. Strangers again, although linked forever by a chain of dead men and women whose ultimate fate they had once held in their hands. Accomplices in crime, or as Leonard preferred to think, retribution.

He'd half expected it when the Bureau's new assignment fell into his lap.

He'd reached for the Port Authority locker and opened the compartment to find the customary folder. He pulled the yellow envelope out with a heavy heart already knowing whose photograph it would contain.

Ramona's.

Their instincts had been right. You weren't allowed to leave the crime scene with impunity. There was always a price to pay.

He sighed.

He wandered home. In no hurry.

As usual, the dossier he was provided with was limited but to the point.

Her name.

Her location.

Revealed nothing about her life, who she was or had been, let alone the fact that she had seemingly been running the organisation and was now a deserter of sorts. A traitor?

It appeared she had fled to New Orleans and was now staying at an Airbnb in the Vieux Carré in New Orleans, a block from Ramparts. The Bureau was nothing but ruthlessly efficient when it came to locating its targets. She had cut her hair in a bob and changed its colour but she was still easily identifiable from the set of photos taken from a distance by whoever had pinned her down in her Louisiana hideaway. An airline boarding pass in his name was clipped to the pages of the thin dossier. The reservation code was appended so that he might book his return flight as and when the job was completed. There were a couple of local telephone numbers provided where he could find assistance should he require weaponry or anything necessary when he arrived in town. The Bureau always thought of everything.

A room had been booked at the St Marie Hotel, off Bourbon Street for him under an assumed name, and the relevant false I.D. provided, so there would be nothing to connect the air passenger with the tourist.

He kept Ramona under observation for 48 hours to ensure she was alone and had not travelled here with anyone. He watched her from a distance as she shopped, walked up and down the French Quarter, ambled down the Mississippi shore and ate at the Acme Oyster Bar and the Pearl. Always on her own.

She wore jeans and assorted sweatshirts, low-heeled ballerina shoes and a quirky Panama hat during daytime, which she replaced by a baseball cap in the evenings.

She seemed happy enough.

On occasions she would halt and look back, as if somehow aware she was being followed, but Leonard kept well out of sight.

He was waiting for the right opportunity but was also in no real hurry. The Bureau had not given any kind of time limit to complete the job.

It rained.

Often, when the rain falls in New Orleans, the heavens open and torrents descend from the sky, rivers of water flooding the gutters, like a punishment from the heaven and you have to take shelter or you will be soaked to the bone and left shaken by the sheer ferocity of the assault. Then, just a few minutes later, the clouds have miraculously moved on and the sun is out again in all its regal splendour, and the water as if by magic evaporates, melts away, leaving thin volutes of steam rising from the pavement, and the smell of the city envelops you like a shroud, stale beer, crawfish boil spices, the odour of the mighty river nearby all combining into something unique, while your shirt dries, sticking to your skin like a shrinking shroud.

He'd been following her down Canal Street. She had taken refuge from the downpour under the awning of a movie house, and on the other side of the road, he had found shelter between the swinging doors of a large department store.

Distracted by the ferocity of the elements, Leonard had briefly taken his eyes off her, as he squeezed himself between the heavy doors, jostling with a few others with the same thought. When he looked up again, he saw her by the movie house, standing still and staring straight in his direction.

They exchanged distant glances.

Recognised each other but made no attempt to communicate, knowing conversation was now useless.

There was no turning back.

That night, she dined at The Gumbo Shop, and following her meal took the direction to Jackson Square and crossed the railway tracks and reached the riverbank. He followed her, a hundred yards separating them, although she knew he was there, tracking her.

She'd changed into a dress, carried no handbag.

Past the parked riverboats with their now silent euphoniums, she now made her way towards the big Mall, past the Monument to the Immigrant and finally stopped by the Aquarium, found a stone bench facing the river and sat herself down.

He caught up with her.

She looked up.

'Of course, it would be you they sent, wouldn't it?' she said quietly.

He nodded.

He didn't know what to say, how to convey his feelings at this point and make it meaningful. He remained silent.

'Make it painless. And dignified ...' Ramona asked.

'I will.'

And he did, her lifeless body later abandoned in the swamp of a nearby bayou, never to be seen again.

12
Love Will Tear Me Apart

Several years had gone by.

Leonard was still killing. Rather unfortunately, the Bureau seemed to assign him to the despatch of women. By now he had wearily grown used to it

It was just a job.

Which didn't make him the devil, nor a man of wealth and taste. On the rare occasions these days that he allowed himself to give the matter undue thought, he maybe saw himself as a benevolent angel of death.

He killed the people other killers preferred to steer clear of.

Someone had to do it.

He justified his job by always reminding himself that he carried out his work tasks with kindness, There was no extraneous pain involved; no torture or lingering agony for the unfortunate victim to contend with. He took no joy in completing his assignments. He found no pleasure in the killing. It's what the Bureau paid him for. On the dot. And he was good at it by now. Precise, decisive, clean.

He killed women on occasion.

There was no element of hate or misogyny involved, just an acceptance of the fact that were he not to do so, there were other operatives who would and they more likely than not would make a mess of it, falter in their aim out of sentimentality, botch things up and leave the mark in writhing pain, bleeding away, her mind filled with despair, her body torn asunder by terrible pain and abominable thoughts coursing through her brain as the light and consciousness ebbed away all too slowly. Until the light died and pain was no longer and, who knew, maybe some feeling of peace beyond thought or existence.

He allowed his victims dignity, even in death.

His weapon of choice had become a SIG Sauer P229 Elite Compact, which he preferred to use at close range, when possible, and without a suppressor.

Unbiased observers might think that Leonard had a cold heart, but they would have been wrong. He now owned an indifferent heart. He would never kill a child, he knew, though the possibility had fortunately never occurred. And on a world scale, was he not just an insignificant element in the front of evil that dominated the headlines: drug wars, civil wars, military wars, school killings, needless crimes daily, ethnic cleansing … The list was an endless one.

Beyond the job he had somehow inherited or fallen into, he was at heart a gentle man. He still loved books and music and, when alone on what was now his permanent SoHo apartment, he would play music all day long, while he read his books. His musical tastes had initially been traditionally classical, the romantics, Berlioz, Grieg, Debussy, Satie. Then in his late teens he had experienced the flowering of folk music and only came to rock'n'roll when Bob Dylan went electric and never looked back. Some songs and melodies were capable of moving him to the point of tears, Joy Division, R.E.M., the Incredible String Band, Bridget St John, the Walkabouts, A Flock of Seagulls, the Flying Lizards, his tastes were similarly eclectic and admirable.

In outward appearance, he tried to blend in, carefully dressing balanced between ordinariness and the minor reaches of whatever fashion was trending, but never far enough to be noticed. He remembered Hopley's admonitions. Your reliable everyday killer for hire. The Bureau had come to trust him implicitly, he knew, although at the back of his mind lurked a constant question mark, an eagerness to know who else might, in the shadows, be also working for them. Although thoughts of revenge against whoever had despatched Meg were now a thing of the past. Impractical.

He had learned never to ask why a particular person was a chosen target. It had no bearing on things. He had killed men too, of course. Leonard was an equal opportunity executioner but had somehow become the first choice when it came to eliminating women. The go-to guy. Accordingly, the Bureau would afford him some leeway, which meant that he was now allowed to decline jobs in certain cities, in no small part dictated by the fact he preferred not to return to a scene of crime within at least 18 months of a hit. Or if the assignment might entail missing out on a concert he wished to attend at Webster Hall or a gig that appealed downtown in the Village. As time went by, music was becoming more of a priority to Leonard than death.

The city slept, restless souls gathered in its web. The lost and the found, the good and the bad, the grey and the black because only the sheets in which they are tangled could afford to stay white, and even then only occasionally.

Helen at 3a.m. Wandering the streets in a daze. Emerging from University Place and making her way towards Washington Square and Sullivan Street. A night without stars or clouds, just a blanket with all the colours of darkness. The arch is illuminated and looks cinematically artificial. The fountain is empty. A flutter of breeze timidly slithers between the trees. The squirrels, whose domain it is, and which she often feeds at the weekend, are nowhere to be seen and she wonders where they all stay or hide at this time of night.

She is aware she has crossed an invisible line. And that there is no going back.

Her mind flashes back to her early days in New York, the dancing gig at the Continental Ballroom, the kindness of Leonard, the lies. She desperately needed the money and had agreed to Patrice's offer to disappear and cut off all links to Leonard. They had paid for her journey to L.A. and provided her with a useful introduction. That had been her second mistake.

Initially, Helen had travelled to New York, like so many others before her in search of an impossible dream. It hadn't worked out. The Continental took such a heavy percentage when she redeemed her dance tickets and she knew she would never manage to make enough to pay any rent, let alone feed and clothe herself properly.

But L.A. was no better. She had thought she could survive juggling menial jobs at first, some waitressing at an Italian diner and a late-night shift at the bar at a joint close to LAX. It didn't work out. So, she took her pride in hand and got in touch with Patrice's contact, as a last resort, assuring herself it would just be a temporary fix and that no one she knew would ever recognise her out here in California.

She knew she had a decent body and was reasonably good looking. The way men looked at her confirmed this. She was tall and rangy, and with the right clothes could attract attention easily, mid-size natural tits holding high, thin in the waist but curvy enough below and with a dancer's legs. And Helen had always had something of an exhibitionist streak; always the first at summer camp to shed her clothes and lead the skinny-dipping rush into the still-cold lake. Maybe she had thought she could dance this way for a couple of years, save some money, even study a little in her spare time, and learn some stuff that would lead her by her mid-20s to a more promising career stream.

And, oh how she enjoyed the actual dancing! Free of the often-clumsy partners back at the Continental in the early days, and their octopus-like wandering hands. Just her. Her body. On stage, In the glare of the lights. Where she was the star of her own movie. So what if she had to do it in the nude? It was only flesh, skin, and if men paid handsomely to watch, where was the damn harm?

She spent days preparing mix tapes. Adding tracks, deleting others, reinstating some and desperately trying to recall tunes she had danced to in high school back home or heard on the radio but the titles and performers of which she had failed to note. The club was in West Hollywood, down a badly-lit side street, neon sign outside flashing intermittently. She was initially booked for two shifts, one in late afternoon and another at night when the tips were more generous, she was assured, but newbies had to pay their dues and keep the stage busy in the fallow hours.

She rehearsed in front of the full-length bathroom mirror. Agonized whether she should merely trim her pubic hair or dispense with it altogether. After much deliberation, she opted for the former, if only because she was aware her outer labia were slightly fleshy and she would feel overly self-conscious if she displayed them without a protective if ephemeral curtain of curls.

She could edit three songs into each set, each echoing the continuous shedding of her clothes until she was fully exposed and lost in dance to the sounds, with the middle tune of necessity slower, to accompany the time wrapping her long white limbs around the pole. Helen was mighty nervous as she had never done pole work before and had lied about it in the interview. She'd wing it. And if her gyratory gymnastics around the cold metal pole might initially be lacking in poise and dynamics, she was confident the music she was cavorting to would soothe the thoughts and loins of the male audience. Velvet Underground, Chris Isaak, John Cale, Terry Reid, Lou Reed and Television would underpin her set, she decided, and she would twirl under the naked glare of the coloured spotlight, her mind and limbs in thrall to the heartbeat of the bass, the wail of electric guitars and the doo-doo-doo-doo doos of the girls harmonizing along.

It now feels like it happened ages ago.

It was easy money. If you swallowed the sense of shame.

A year later, she had moved back to New York, working in another club owned by the same shadowy proprietors. Just a cog in their network, a face, a cunt, a pair of tits. Has she held onto her dignity? Helen is uncertain.

But she now knows as she walks through the park that she is on a slippery slope.

She feels dizzy, the night's cold hair like a slap in the face.

A week ago she had broken one of her initial vows. She'd insisted from the very outset of her time in the clubs that she would never consent to private lap dances. Nor would she sleep with customers. She was of course asked on a continual basis. But she had stuck to her principles. The last shred of her dignity.

Until now.

The man was rougher than she expected and out of fear and resignation, having crossed that terrible Rubicon, she hadn't had the energy, the will power to ask him to stop as he relentlessly, loudly pounded her, extracting agonized moans from her throat, which he no doubt mistook for sounds of pleasure.

She feels dirty.

Her only relief is that she didn't do it for the money, although he had been continuously showering her with small gifts in his steady rite of seduction. First flowers, then an expensive cashmere wrap, and finally jewellery. She knows so little about the latter, whether it's cheap or valuable. Fake or real.

And, against her better judgment, she had given in.

Yes, she had appetites and took some form of wicked pleasure knowing she could arouse men. Not that any woman standing stark naked and exposed on a stage with the glare of powerful spotlights accentuating the fragility and highlights of her flesh could easily turn on a guy.

She had agreed to have a drink with him. He was coarse, not the sort of man who would normally attract her. Shorter than her, over-cologned, articulate about his desires rather than his actual words. Someone she had little in common with. But her damn curiosity had condemned her. There had been a few, meaningless encounters since her night with Leonard, but nothing of significance, always one-night stands with no names exchanged or the will to repeat. From the moment she had first wondered 'What if?' when he had casually revealed he was well acquainted with the Lou Reed song she had earlier stripped to and even met the artist a few times.

'I love that song,' he had said. 'But you know it's all about trannies?' He did have a wicked smile. 'But I know that I'm safe with you, ain't I darling? You don't have any bad surprises lurking down there, have you? You're the real thing. You've shown me and a thousand others the goods already. You can't lie on stage, can you?' He chortled.

They'd been sitting in a sheltered alcove in a late-might speakeasy close to Alphabet City; Helen was in civilian garb, wearing a short denim skirt and a T-shirt with a Rolling Stones Sticky Fingers logo. Her winter coat was a pick-up from Goodwill's, all khaki and green military patterns. He wore a thin gold chain around his neck. Later, once he has assumed ownership, he will buy her a gold ankle chain and insist she wear it at all times, even on stage. But now, his leer both attracted and repelled her. She felt like prey to a snake, drawing her closer, ready to devour her. She had never known bad men and curiosity killed the cat.

She agreed to visit his apartment, a plush open-plan loft overlooking the Hudson River. The first time he fucked her, he took her from behind crushing her body against the plate glass window as she giddily watched the lights of New Jersey glimmer like distant stars while she endured his thrusts.

'I love ya, babe,' he said as he came with a caveman's grunt. 'You're fuckin' mine now.'

He had offered to call her an Uber, but Helen wanted to walk back home, collect her thoughts, resigned to her new situation in the knowledge she had made a bad mistake. She hadn't showered, his seed still inside her, he had taken her raw and she would have to take a pill the following morning, and when she reached Bleecker Street she began to cry, now feeling so terribly alone, as if she had cheated on herself, betrayed who she was.

Leonard was between jobs and restless.

At his third-floor window, looking out over Wooster Street. 3 a.m. He should be sleeping, reading, watching something on

TV, anything, but was unable to get his mind to focus on anything. Thoughts crowded each other out. The faces of men and women past. His all-too-familiar ghosts. Haunting him, reproaching him. Those he had killed. His roll of death. Those he had done wrong by.

A movement in the shadows on the cobbled street. Almost in slow motion, a young woman, tall, rangy, in a tight fitting back T-shirt and denim skirt, a shapeless coat draped across her right shoulder. Long legs. Ballet shoes. Leonard squinted: braless. Her auburn hair a mass of untamed curls. From his vantage point at the window, he is unable to make out the colour of her eyes. Blue is his guess. But there is something weirdly familiar about her. She walks slowly, her face a study in concentration, visibly in distress, crying maybe? She appears in no hurry to reach whatever destination she is bound for, her feet delicately skimming the pavement as she makes her way down Spring, oblivious to her surroundings. Like an Eadweard Muybridge model whose movements have been deconstructed.

Like a flash of lightning, it comes to him.

Helen.

From the Port Authority, the Continental, that one feverish night in his hotel room, his bed.

Yes. It's definitely her.

Slightly older.

Sadder.

His phantom lady, the one who might hold the key to how the madness that became his life was triggered.

Leonard's heart skips a beat. The spectres of his past victims crowding the room where he stands, pinned to the ground, instantly evaporate.

He wants to call out to her, somehow catch her attention. But the window won't open. There is a safety lock and after he had purchased the apartment from the travelling academic who had decided not to return to the States, somehow the keys had never been located. In summer, the A/C sufficed and in winter there was no need to ever open the window anyway.

He brushes his finger against the glass. Peers into the growing darkness as the young woman moves out of the impoverished circle of clarity she has briefly inhabited as she passes the streetlight. He raps on the window harder in an effort to catch her attention. A yellow cab rushes down the street. She turns her head slightly. Toward him? Toward the speeding car? Looks up at his window, as of sensing his presence. He is overcome with shame; in the surrounding penumbra of Wooster Street in the dead of night would she think he was some kind of creep, a flasher? Some Hitchcock voyeur out of a bad noir movie? Can she even see him properly, let alone recognise him? The light is on in the apartment's front room that looks out onto Wooster and he must be just a dark shadow to her he reasons; a blur at most. She looks away. Moves on. An eerie night vision, an Edward Hopper-like picture of loneliness and beauty.

She walks out of sight.

Leonard hurriedly slips on a jacket and steps into his shoes, opens his door and rushes down the stairs in too much of a rush to wait for the elevator.

He almost stumbles as he emerges onto Wooster Street. Runs down towards the corner with Spring, hoping to catch another look at her, make sure it is actually Helen or just a look-alike. Glances left, right and centre but there is no sign of the young, distressed woman. How come? She wasn't even walking fast. Could she, by utmost coincidence, live nearby, have disappeared through her own front door? The streets are empty in all directions.

Leonard takes a deep breath.

Had he imagined her?

Had he willed her to appear, from out of the past?

It hurts. Badly. It made no sense, but there you are.

Could the man at the window have any idea that less than two hours ago, she was being unceremoniously fucked overlooking the Hudson River and that she still carried the evidence inside her cunt? Of course not. But the shame was overwhelming. She had whored herself out. And cheaply at that. What had come over her? She couldn't even remember the damn guy's name.

Her next set at Jimmy's was not until the following Tuesday. She was booked in for six days in a row; both afternoon and evening sessions.

She jumped into the shower and cleansed herself thoroughly of the man, banishing his tobacco and booze breath from her skin, rubbing herself pink. And took a morning after pill.

In cinematic slow motion, drifting as in a dream, Helen moved to her bed and curled up, pulling the quilt up to her chin and lay there, daydreaming, confused, ashamed. She had made mistakes before, but this time, it felt like something different, something worse. She had betrayed herself and it left a bad sting reverberating across her mind. And there was no way of making it better, erasing the memory, the bad sex. It was something she would now have to live with forever. She took a deep breath, closed her eyes and sought the solace of sleep. But even when it arrived, it didn't help. Bad mistake. Truly.

Her unfortunate new lover was back on Tuesday, propping up the bar, clapping over-enthusiastically as she stripped mechanically, making it openly clear she was now his girl. He'd brought a bottle of champagne along, under the mistaken assumption it gave him a touch of class. And was waiting for her at the back door after she had changed into civilian garb.

'You're coming with me.'

It was an order, not an invitation.

She tried to make excuses, but he would have nothing of it. On her final night of the week's stint at the club, he gifted her with the thin gold anklet and enjoined her to wear it on a permanent basis.

Barely a week later and having used her every single night since her surrender, he demanded she move in with him, and she did not have the courage to resist, but also kept the payments up on her shared rental downtown, leaving some of her personal belongings there. He still tolerated her working at Jimmy's, which allowed her a modicum of financial independence as he now insisted in a grand gesture of largesse on paying for everything: food, new clothes, expensive restaurants, accessories. Gleefully showing off his new possession. He never appeared to do any work, and Helen found it wise not to ask any questions.

She began saving for a rainy day, as she knew deep inside either he would tire of her fast enough and move on to his next prey, or she would inevitably strain too far at all the restrictions he was imposing on her, his brutal possessiveness, his crudeness. If the latter, she feared his response.

Once, she had found pleasure in her dancing, a sense of pride in the shameless flaunting of her body, the way her limbs embraced the music as she moved to its languorous beat, every movement and moment resonating deep inside her, oblivious to her audience, ignoring their collective lust. It was a celebration of her beauty, her powers of seduction. Now her joy had gone and her performances were mechanical, just muscle memory.

She felt like a captive in an old black and white movie full of clichés, the gangster's moll. He was a bad man, she knew. She was often there, sitting politely on the sofa when he held meetings, unavoidably listening to his telephone calls, his plans. She found out he had a sizeable investment and part control of the club where she danced and its affiliated sites across the country, which explained some of the shady goings-on in the back room, the small envelopes changing hands, the drugs being openly peddled in full sight. Helen found out she was not the first dancer he had been involved with. There were dark whispers about her predecessor, a Ukrainian beauty with thoroughbred looks that had far outshone her artistic talents. Something had caused her departure. Some said she had been removed to another city and was now being whored, even.

Out of the blue, one day, she was approached in front of the Angelika, on the corner of Houston and Mercer. An undercover law officer who was fully aware of her relationship with the bad man, asking for her cooperation. She had agreed to provide information. Not so much out of civic duty, but out of spite, of anger at the way she had been reeled into the abyss.

Helen had known the risks she was taking.

She began to listen more attentively to his calls, taking furtive notes thereafter. Agreed to accompany him to outside meetings, stored compromising information she had picked up on. Maybe it might prove a way out, a chance to rid herself of him before matters got worse?

He asked her to sleep with another man. A favour, he called it, implying she owed him this service. Just the once, he said. A friend who was on the run and had need of a woman, and hiring an escort for the occasion might be taking too much of a risk. Helen reluctantly agreed and then leaked the fugitive's location to her handler. By the time they pounced, though, he had moved on, so it was all for nothing. Encouraged by her docility, her bad man lover arranged a threesome with another of his made friends. Helen had never been with two men before. He was aggressively vocal as he watched, and filmed her being mounted by the stranger. Later, as they drank, she had to tiptoe her way to the bathroom and wretch. Not so much disgusted by what they had done to her but by her cowardice and acceptance of this new, twisted state of affairs. The two men never even noticed her discomfort and kept bantering about her and her prowess in bed as if she was not even present. They insisted she watch with them the short clip of her being pounded at both ends and Helen was sick again. They laughed. Later, when they momentarily left the room to visit the hotel's bar downstairs to celebrate, Helen rapidly inserted a memory stick into the second man's phone and, the following day, slipped it to the cop who was had become her handler.

'We are fully aware you no longer prefer not to take on assignments in the city proper,' the voice now speaking for the Bureau explained. 'But we would ask you to make an exception.'

Leonard nodded. As they were speaking over the phone, it mattered not but over the years he had reached a sort of silent understanding with his invisible employers, a degree of familiarity now rather than a relationship of employer and now senior killing lackey.

'It's where I happen to live. Involves more risks. Never shit where you eat, as they say.'

'We know the saying. We believe in it too.'

Just voices over the telephone. They still had never met. Never would. Rules of the game. This was how their business was conducted. Never in person. Ramona had been an exception. So long ago now, he realised. Commission. Delivery of locker key. Dossier. Payments made to offshore accounts.

'This particular matter has a degree of urgency.'

'I'm still not sure,' Leonard said.

'We can make it worth your while to make this one exception to your rules.'

'Why me?'

'Because you complete jobs other operatives have qualms about.'

'Ah, a woman.'

'And the man she consorts with. She betrayed him but he was the one who made the mistake of trusting her. A terrible breach.'

'You know I have no interest in the reasons for the hit,' Leonard reminded the voice on the other end of the line.

'So? We'll double your fee if you can resolve the problem within the week.'

It had been a couple of months since his last assignment and he was feeling restless. Ever since he had caught a glimpse of the young woman who could have been Helen, his ghost of Wooster Street, he had made attempts to find her. To no avail. How many tall redheads with curly hair and a ballet dancer's walk could there be in the city? And maybe she didn't even live in Manhattan, had been just a tourist finding her way through the SoHo night?

He had tried. A few false leads: once catching sight of someone with similar characteristics waiting to board a train to the burbs at Grand Central Station, only to find when he caught up with her that she was nothing like his all-too-brief apparition.

Leonard kept on wondering what had made her so special, tugged on his heartstrings and loins from the memory of half a dozen clumsy dances and a brief night of lust? Then walked out of his life. Until now?

Damned if he knew any more.

It made no sense, this obsession.

Organising a new hit, a double one, would clear his mind, focus on real life, banish her maybe forever, Leonard thought.

So he accepted the job.

There was no time for a dossier so he was briefed over the phone.

'He's connected, but is not known to normally carry,' Leonard was told. He wrote down a name and an address. Peered closely at the photo that had been messaged on to him, then deleted it. 'He owns a stake in a local strip club and is shacked up with one of the dancers. She's your main target. Her next shift is Saturday night. We don't have a pic of her, but she's a skinny, tallish redhead, but with natural tits for a change seeing her profession. That should narrow it down for you. The two of them normally leave the club together. Hit them then. No need for discretion.'

'Half now, half on completion,' he said.

'As usual.'

'Done deal.' The line went dead and he put the phone down. He'd been standing by his window, looking out on Wooster Street. Again. It had become a bad habit.

The week before Christmas weather had arrived in Manhattan with a stark vengeance.

Leonard stood in the shadows across the street from Jimmy's, observing the comings and goings under the awning of a Korean deli, filtering out the sounds of music leaking out; at one stage recognising the chorus of Lou Reed's 'Walk on the Wild Side' and humming along.

He drew his overcoat's collar tight around his neck; he should have brought a scarf to protect him from the growing cold.

Finally, the bouncers waved the die-hard customers away and the club's flickering neon sign was switched off. Half an hour later, he recognised the mobster as he left the joint. He was followed, as if reluctantly, by a thin woman wrapped in an army trench coat, trailing a foot or so behind him. She must be the dancer.

The couple made their way down the block and turned into an unattended street parking lot.

As they approached a metal grey BMW, Leonard quickly crossed the street and as an electronic ping sounded and the car's parking lights flashed on and off, drew his gun. He shot the man first in the back of the head and adjusted his stance to bring the woman into focus. The guy crumpled to the ground and in the same moment, the dancer turned toward Leonard. The sudden glimpse of her face was a dagger to Leonard's heart. But his finger was already squeezing the trigger and the bullet punctured her heart before she could say a single word, eyes wide open, terror spreading through Helen's consciousness until the curtain fell. She slowly stumbled against the side of the car before sliding down slowly to the parking lot ground like a marionette being reeled down by its strings.

Leonard lingered a moment, his whole world in total disarray even as his nervous system screamed at him to flee before the gunshots attracted any possible witness.

Helen.

Leonard hadn't cried since childhood. But he did now as he looked one final time at her face, now in repose and strangely peaceful.

Finally, he forced himself to face away and just as he did snow began to fall on Manhattan.

A few days later, on Christmas Eve, Leonard hanged himself.

ABOUT THE AUTHOR

Maxim Jakubowski worked for several decades in publishing and later owned the Murder One bookshop. He has written 20 novels (including 10 under a collaborative pen name, several of which made the *Sunday Times* top 10) and 5 collections of short stories.

He is recognised as a major expert on popular fiction and reviewed crime for 12 years each for *Time Out London* and *The Guardian*, and won several awards in the mystery and SF & fantasy field.

He is also a major editor of bestselling anthologies, and has been translated widely. He lives in London.

Also available from this author

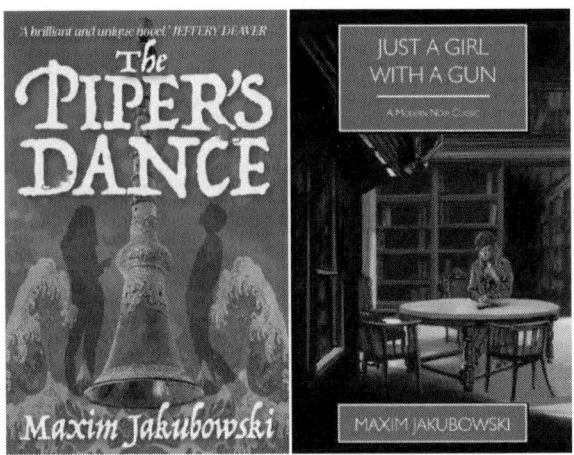